AFTER
ELI

AFTER ELI

Rebecca Rupp

CANDLEWICK PRESS

Copyright © 2012 by Rebecca Rupp

"Nothing Gold Can Stay" from the book THE POETRY OF ROBERT FROST edited by Edward Connery Lathem. Copyright © 1923, 1969 by Henry Holt and Company, copyright © 1951 by Robert Frost. Reprinted by permission of Henry Holt and Company, LLC.

First paperback edition 2015

The Library of Congress has cataloged the hardcover edition as follows:

Rupp, Rebecca.
After Eli / Rebecca Rupp. — 1st ed.
p.   cm.
Summary: After the death of his older brother, Daniel Anderson became engrossed in recording details about dead people, how they died, and whether their deaths mattered, but he is eventually drawn back into interaction with the living.
ISBN 978-0-7636-5810-6 (hardcover)
[1. Death — Fiction. 2. Interpersonal relations — Fiction.
3. Books and reading — Fiction. 4. Brothers — Fiction.] I. Title.
PZ7.R8886Aft 2012
[Fic] — dc23   2011048344

ISBN 978-0-7636-7674-2 (paperback)

15 16 17 18 19 20 BVG 10 9 8 7 6 5 4 3 2 1

Printed in Berryville, VA, U.S.A.

This book was typeset in Warnock.

Candlewick Press
99 Dover Street
Somerville, Massachusetts 02144

visit us at www.candlewick.com

For all the families left behind

ELI ALAN ANDERSON (April 25, 1981–April 16, 2004)

Killed in Iraq by a bomb.

It's been over a year since I last heard from Isabelle.

She sent me a postcard a couple months after she left, the way people do when they're pretending they're going to stay in touch, and I remember taking it out of our beat-up mailbox at the end of the road, and how the sight of her swoopy handwriting in red fountain pen made my heart beat faster for a minute. Isabelle always writes in red so that all her days will be red-letter days, and she uses a fountain pen because it's elegant.

Elegant was always one of Isabelle's words.

Today the mail was a couple of bills and a school-teacher magazine for my mom and a flyer for a sale on fence posts at Tractor Supply, which looked like a good deal if you happened to want fence posts. Nothing from Isabelle.

I still have that postcard though. It has a big full moon on the front, the picture side, with a bunch of little animals dancing in front of it. A couple of rabbits and a dog and a cat and a cow. On the back she wrote, "Looks like us, doesn't it? Remember the Moon Elves!" with a couple of kisses that didn't mean anything and then her name.

Isabelle.

I remember the Moon Elves.

I remember everything about the summer Isabelle was here.

CHAPTER 1

GEORGE MALLORY (1886–1924)
Died climbing Mount Everest.
....
Daniel (E.) Anderson's Book of the Dead

My name wasn't always Daniel (E.) Anderson. My real middle name, the one on the birth certificate in the fireproof box in the back of my mom's closet, is James. I added the (E.) after my brother, Eli, died.

There's this tribe in Paraguay that whenever somebody dies, everybody changes their name so that the dead person's ghost can't come back and find them. But I put Eli's name in mine as a way of keeping him around. Not that I would ever tell anybody that now, because it sounds dumb. It sounds like the sort of thing girls do when they run around wearing their boyfriends' sweaters. But I was only a kid then and I didn't know crap.

I like to think that now that I'm older, I understand why Eli did what he did, which ended up getting him killed. Though I guess I'll never really know, not all the way. Walter says that human motivations are complicated, and that when it comes right down to it, nobody knows all the reasons we do the things we do. Most of the time we don't even know ourselves. But I didn't know Walter then, and what I mostly felt about Eli, way deep down, was mad as hell. Dying was his own damn fault is what I thought, and now look at the life he'd stuck me with.

I used to think Eli was like George Mallory, the mountain climber guy. I've seen these old pictures of Mallory on the Internet, and in a couple he even looks a little bit like Eli. Mallory got killed in 1924 climbing Mount Everest, which he set out to do *because it was there.* That's what he actually said when people asked him why he wanted to climb the world's tallest mountain. Walter, who reads everything, once told me that "because it's there" are probably the three most famous words in the history of mountain climbing, which indicates to me that mountain-climbing history could sure use some better words.

Anyway, that was the end of Mallory. His freeze-dried body was found on Everest's north face in 1999 with a broken leg and a hole in the skull. Nobody knows if he died while he was still going up or while he was on the way back down, so he may never have made it to the top of the world's highest mountain at all. Which would really suck.

But face it, *because it's there* is a dumb reason for getting killed. I wonder how Mallory's wife and kids felt about him batting off to the Himalayas to climb some stupid mountain and leaving them on their own. When he left for India or Nepal or wherever, his oldest daughter, Clare, was only nine. That's younger than I was when Eli died.

Eli got killed in Iraq on April 16, 2004. The truck he was in ran over an Improvised Explosive Device, which is one of those bombs they bury along the side of the road. They sent him home in a coffin with a flag.

I was eleven then, and I'd been waiting for Eli

to come home so we could see *The Return of the King.* He'd taken me to see *The Fellowship of the Ring* and *The Two Towers,* but *The Return of the King* wasn't being released until after his tour of duty in Iraq started. So we had a pact that we'd wait until we could see it together, even though by then it wouldn't be in the theaters anymore and we'd have to watch it at home on DVD.

All through the funeral and everything, I kept thinking how Eli was looking forward to that movie and how now he'd never see how it all came out in the end. Eli really liked those movies.

Except for the elves. He thought the elves were dorks.

Practically the whole town came to Eli's funeral. Almost everybody from his old high-school class was there, and most of their parents, and all the teachers, and Mr. Bingham, the principal. Chuck Bowers, the football coach, was there, and all the guys on the Catamounts football team that Eli used to be captain of his senior year, dressed up in navy-blue Sunday suits that looked too tight around the collar. Even without their shoulder pads, they were way too big for the funeral parlor's little folding metal chairs.

Mr. Corrigan closed the hardware store for the afternoon, and he and all his employees came, because Eli used to work there part-time in the summers. And Bev and her husband, Roy, came, who own Bev's Caf, the restaurant in town, where Eli's picture is up on the wall. And then there were all the neighbors and a lot of relatives and Eli's college buddies, and his girlfriend, Rachel Crowley, who cried so hard that you could hear her above the organist playing "Stairway to Heaven."

What I remember about that funeral is how my aunt Wendy made me wear a tie. Aunt Wendy was pretty much in charge at Eli's funeral because my mom was stuffed full of sedatives and my dad was wandering around like a zombie. The slow, dumb kind of zombie, not the fast kind with the teeth. He was in shock, is what people said.

"I don't want to wear a tie," I said.

"Stand still, Daniel," Aunt Wendy said, making a lunge for my throat.

Aunt Wendy works for the U.S. Post Office. She is the size that women's clothing stores call "queenly," and Eli used to say that Aunt Wendy in her regulation blue Bermuda shorts was about as scary a sight as he'd ever seen, even counting the part in *Alien* where the monster jumps out of the guy's chest.

"I won't," I said.

I kept thinking how Eli would have teased me about wearing a tie, poking me in the ribs and saying who did I think I was, Donald Trump? But Eli wasn't there. All that was left of him was in a six-foot box. I didn't want to think about what was in that box.

"Eddie, please," Aunt Wendy called, holding up the tie and waggling it in the air. "Just give me a minute over here. I can't do a thing with him."

Eddie is my dad, but only Aunt Wendy calls him that.

"Christ," my dad said.

He jerked the tie around my neck and tied it with a twist that reminded me how he and my aunt Wendy and uncle Al had been raised on a farm in Ohio, where they used to kill their own chickens.

"Don't make things harder for your mother than they already are," my dad said.

Though it seemed to me my mom was pretty much okay, being next to unconscious.

"Go sit down and behave yourself," my dad said, giving me a little shove.

Right then I wished my dad had been the one to run over a bomb.

Lots of people talked at Eli's funeral. Mr. Bingham, the principal, called him "the best and the brightest," and Coach Bowers said that they sure broke the mold when they made Eli. Pastor Jay, the minister from the Methodist church where Eli and I went to Sunday school, talked about how the Lord works in mysterious ways, and Miss Myrna Walker, who was Eli's favorite teacher back in high school, said a poem.

"Nature's first green is gold,
Her hardest hue to hold.
Her early leaf's a flower;
But only so an hour.

Then leaf subsides to leaf.
So Eden sank to grief,
So dawn goes down to day.
Nothing gold can stay."

Her voice cracked up a little when she came to that last line, and all of a sudden, even though I've always thought that poetry was pretty much crap, my eyes stung and my throat tightened up so that it hurt under that stupid tie.

Then the pallbearers stood up — my uncle Al and Jim Pilcher, who was Eli's best friend from high school, and Rachel Crowley's brother Jason, and Coach Bowers, and a couple of the college guys. Coach Bowers gave Eli's coffin a pat before he helped pick it up, and let his hand rest there a minute on Eli's flag, gentle, like he did sometimes on a football player's shoulder after he'd played a really good game.

Then we drove to the cemetery in a long train of cars following the hearse, and they folded up the flag on the coffin and gave it to my mom, and that was the last of Eli.

Afterward, people came back to our house and hung around downstairs eating all the lasagnas and macaroni casseroles and pies that neighbors had brought us, as if dying was something you could fix with carbs. I didn't want to talk to anybody and I didn't want any stupid macaroni casserole. So I left and went up to my room, that's across the hall from the room that used to be Eli's.

Eli's door was closed, so I could almost pretend that he was in there, reading or drawing or playing computer games or listening to music. There was a sign on his door that said KEEP OUT and underneath in red marker a P.S. that said DANNY YOU TWERP THIS MEANS YOU TOO! Though if I knocked, he pretty much always let me come in.

I stood there holding my breath and wishing that this was all just a lousy dream and that any minute I'd wake up. I thought that maybe if I held my breath and wished hard enough and knocked, Eli would answer. But I didn't knock, because there wasn't any light under Eli's door and I knew it wasn't a dream.

That's when I started my Book of the Dead.

I still have it, though I don't write in it anymore. It's in an old three-ring binder of Eli's that he had his freshman year in college. There used to be a label on it that said *Physics 01 Bates Bldg. Room 22,* but I peeled that off.

The real Book of the Dead is from ancient Egypt. It's this collection of magic spells that are supposed to help a dead person make it safely from the world of the living to the afterlife, which wasn't easy in ancient Egypt. You had to protect yourself from hostile entities and placate the gods and fight off supernatural crocodiles. Actually the ancient Egyptian death trip sounded a lot like *Dungeons & Dragons.*

There was a final test right at the end. Thoth, the god of wisdom, weighed your heart on a pair of enormous scales, and if it was lighter than a feather, then you were free of sin and you got to go to Egyptian heaven. If it was heavier than the feather, you got eaten by a monster called the Gobbler that was part lion and part hippopotamus.

I wondered what Eli's heart would weigh. I thought Eli had a lot to answer for.

Eli didn't have to go to war. He volunteered. He did it on purpose. I thought how he probably didn't even think about what it would do to us, to me and Mom and Dad and Rachel, if he got killed. He went because he wanted to is what I thought. Because it was there.

So I knew how Clare Mallory felt back in 1924 about her dad, who went up Mount Everest and never came back down. A part of her loved him and missed him and would have done anything to have him back. But a part of her hated him for doing that to her. A part of her was really angry at him too.

CHAPTER 2

CHARLES G. STEPHENS (1862–1920)
Died going over Niagara Falls in a barrel.
....
Daniel (E.) Anderson's Book of the Dead

When I was four or five, I poked a fork into an electrical outlet. The next thing I knew there was a flash and a crack like somebody had whapped me over the head with a frying pan, and then I was lying on the floor with Eli bending over me yelling, "Jesus, Danny, wake up!"

Which is when I knew I'd nearly fried my brains because Eli had taken the Lord's name in vain, which he never did just then because of dating Bridget Babcock, who was a Baptist.

After the fork incident, my mom went out and bought all these little plastic covers and plastered them over every electrical outlet in the house, and

Eli got me this educational picture book called *Safety with Mr. Electricity,* which he used to scare the pants off me. Finally Mom made him stop because I was starting to have nightmares.

In my nightmares Mr. Electricity looked pretty much like the little cartoon guy in the book, with his yellow T-shirt with the lightning bolt on it, except that he had glowy vampire eyes and pointy teeth. At night when the lights were off, he'd crawl out of the electrical outlets and slink around the house, trying to melt the eyeballs of helpless little kids and turn their brains into vegetable soup. Especially helpless little kids who'd poked at his butt with a fork.

After spending my formative years with Eli and Mr. Electricity, it's probably a miracle I can bring myself to charge my iPod.

Anyway, I think it was that fork that gave Eli the idea for his Education Days. I needed them because I was a Darwin Award waiting to happen, is what he said. At first I thought that was a compliment.

Then I found out that actually the Darwin Award is for people who have killed themselves in incredibly stupid ways, thus eliminating themselves from the gene pool. Such as Charles Stephens, who went over Niagara Falls in a barrel with an anvil tied to his feet for ballast. Afterward nothing was left of him but one arm. They knew it was his arm because of the tattoo.

"I think Education Days is a crap idea," I said. "I already go to school. I don't need any more Education Days."

"Admitting you need help is the first step toward solving a problem," Eli said. "This is your chance to benefit from my superior brains and experience. Don't be a wuss."

This was how Eli always talked me into doing things. So far, so as not to be a wuss, I'd jumped off the high board at Marshall Lake, eaten a whole jalapeño pepper, run around the outside of the house naked, called a girl that Eli liked on the phone and pretended to be a computer dating service, and ridden a skateboard down Turkey Hill and into a ditch.

"Forget it, Eli," I said.

"I'm not doing this for you, you twerp," Eli

said. "I'm doing this for me. When the zombies start crawling down the chimney, I don't want you squealing around being short and useless. I want you out there competently defending me, with a cleaver."

Then he gave me this grin, and Eli always had a really great grin, even though it was sort of crooked. It went up higher on one side than the other. That grin always pretty much talked me into doing things too.

Here's some of the stuff Eli taught me on our Education Days:

How to crack my toes.

How to whistle.

Which finger to give when you're giving somebody the finger.

All about bras.

How to smoke a cigarette, even though he told me not to get in the habit because it would rot my lungs.

How to drive a car, even though I could only go fifteen miles per hour up and down the dirt road in back of the barn.

How to unlock a car door with a coat hanger after you've gotten out of the car and slammed the door and left it running with the keys inside it by mistake.

How to shoot a BB gun, what not to shoot it at, and why "Don't fire until you see the whites of their eyes" was a stupid idea.

The seven words that nobody is ever supposed to say and when you can say them anyway.

How to light a barbecue grill in under thirty seconds, using a technique I had to swear never to reveal to Mom or in print.

How to throw a football.

What to do in a fight.

He also told me where babies come from and how to make sure they don't, which pretty much freaked me out at the time, but Eli said give it a few years and I'd realize that there was a lot of potential there.

You'd think that some of this would be the sort of stuff a dad would do, but to tell the truth, a lot of the time our dad wasn't around, and even when he was around, he still wasn't really there, if you know what I mean. Walter says our dad's absence created a vacuum, which is something that Nature abhors, and that Eli filled it up.

Here is a typical conversation without my dad:

....

Scene: *The Anderson family kitchen. In the middle of the room is a large wooden table, on which the OLDER BROTHER once carved his name with a jackknife, which is why the YOUNGER BROTHER was never permitted to have one.*

The MOTHER (Ellen Anderson) is stirring a pot on the stove. The OLDER BROTHER (Eli Anderson, age 17) is sitting on the table with his feet on a chair, eating all the black olives out of the salad bowl. The FATHER (Edward Anderson) is thumping around outside in the garage.

Enter the YOUNGER BROTHER (Danny Anderson, age 6), holding bizarre ceramic object.

Me: Hey, look what I made in school.

Mom (looking over shoulder while stirring): It's lovely, darling.

Eli (dropping olive and clapping hand to heart): That — is — so — *awesome*! Uh . . . what is it? An anteater?

Me (modestly): It's a dragon.

Eli: And it's pink. Way to go, kid. I detect the influence of Picasso and Henri Rousseau and maybe a touch of Captain Underpants.

Me: It was going to be yellow, but Jane-Marie took all the yellow. She made a banana.

Eli: Hey, pink is cool. Lots of good stuff is pink. Like bubble gum and the small intestine and Pamela Anderson's . . .

Mom: *Eli!*

The FATHER (Edward Anderson) enters.

Dad: Get off that table, Eli. It's wobbly enough without you planting your butt on it. You think I've got nothing better to do than patch up the furniture all the time? What's for supper?

Mom: Spaghetti. Look, honey, Danny made a dragon.

Dad: So when are you going to finish stacking that woodpile, Eli? It looks like Paul Bunyan threw up out there.

Eli: I said I'd do it, Dad. I'll do it this weekend.

Me: Dad, did you see my dragon?

Dad: That's a dragon? What kind of dragon is pink? Where's the mail? Did you kids forget to bring in the mail?

....

You see how it was. You'd try to tell him something or show him something but he'd be thinking about something else, like why hadn't you cut the grass or why hadn't you taken your shoes off on the porch because they were all over mud and you were tracking up the floors.

My mom always said that my dad didn't mean it and he just had a lot of worries, and Eli said nobody could grow up with Aunt Wendy without having TSWS and DTMTA. TSWS was Terminal Social Withdrawal Syndrome and DTMTA was Desire to Move to Australia.

But back when I was a kid, having a mostly absent dad didn't bother me all that much because I always had Eli.

I never thought about how I'd get along without Eli being there. In all those Education Days, that's one bit I never learned.

CHAPTER 3

On September 11, 2001, the blue and balmy morning when hijacked planes piloted by Islamist terrorists ripped through the twin towers of New York City's World Trade Center and tore a hole in the Pentagon, America changed forever. On that day we lost our sense of national security and our world became a darker and more dangerous place. Nearly 3,000 people died in the four coordinated suicide attacks, the vast majority in the ruins of the towers, others in the wreckage at the Pentagon and in a rural field near Shanksville, Pennsylvania.

Daniel (E.) Anderson's Book of the Dead

When I think about the terrorist attacks on 9/11, I don't think just about the people who died. I also think about the lucky ones, the people who nearly died but didn't. They missed the plane in Boston or were late to work that morning or had a stomach-ache and decided to stay home sick. They weren't there when the planes hit and so they survived.

Afterward, a lot of them were on the news saying how God must have been looking after them that day. But my question is: Why wasn't God looking after all the passengers on those planes and all the people trapped in the tower on the 106th floor, with the I beams melting under them and the smoke crawling under the doors? Where was God then?

Pastor Jay says there's a pattern behind everything that's just too big for us to understand. But I think he's wrong there. I don't think there's any pattern at all. I think living or dying is just dumb luck. If Eli had taken a few minutes longer to lace up his boots that morning, or if he'd had three eggs for breakfast instead of two, maybe he'd have been in a different truck, one that didn't run over the bomb.

Walter says that every time we make a decision, no matter how small, the universe splits into parallel universes, so that there's a universe where one thing happens and another universe for something else. There are universes where Columbus sank on his way across the Atlantic and where Hitler won World War II. A universe where Eli never went to war, and one where the terrorists never got on the 9/11 planes at all, but decided instead to settle down in Florida and open up a little restaurant on the beach selling crab cakes and French fries and souvenir T-shirts.

"So how come I have to be in this universe?" I said. "How come I can't be in some other one, with Eli still in it?"

Walter said it had something complicated to do with quantum physics.

I was in fourth grade the year the towers went down, and what I remember most about fourth grade is that I had a Hogwarts pencil box, with Harry Potter pencils that had wizards on them, and stars and owls. It's weird after all that's happened how well I can remember that stupid pencil box.

Everything was all Harry Potter that year. Ms. Mellinger, the fourth-grade teacher, had us all divided up into Hogwarts houses for reading and discussion groups, and I was busy hating her because I was in Hufflepuff. Being pissed at Hufflepuff is what I was thinking about on 9/11.

When we first heard about the attacks, I wasn't scared. To tell the truth, I didn't take it in what was going on, any more than all those little kids at the Emma E. Booker Elementary School in Sarasota, Florida, understood right off why the president suddenly got that deer-in-the-headlights expression and stopped reading *The Pet Goat.*

Also I was sort of used to things crashing and blowing up, due to growing up with Eli across the hall blasting virtual orcs on his computer screen all the time.

That night, though, when my mom and dad and I watched the news, it got real. The news guys kept replaying those planes crashing into the towers, with people screaming and crying and running, and the buildings spewing out smoke and then just crumpling down like a house of cards. Crash and fall, over and over.

We heard about the nineteen hijackers with their box cutters, and the staticky voices of people who were about to die making cell phone calls. "We're all gonna die! We're all gonna die!" one woman said. She was so damned scared.

My mom cried and my dad drank Scotch and said a lot of the seven words that nobody is supposed to say. That I was even there shows how upset they were, because usually my mom didn't let me watch stuff like that.

Eli called home in the middle of the third replay of the president talking about evil.

First he talked to Mom and Dad, and from the half I could hear, it didn't sound like he was exactly defusing a traumatic situation.

"No," our mom kept saying. "No. You should be home. We should be together at a time like this."

At which point Dad took the phone because Mom had lost it and needed more Kleenex.

He listened for about six seconds, and then he said, "That's very idealistic of you, Eli, but don't be a fool. You can't do any good there. You want to do something, you go down to the Red Cross and give them a pint of blood or something."

Then he said, "Danny's doing fine."

And then our mom started crying harder, and our dad said, "Now, Ellen, please," and they put me on the phone.

"You doing fine, Dan?" Eli said.

"Are they going to blow us all up?" I said.

"Hell, no," Eli said. But his voice sounded funny.

"Did they kill kids?" I said.

"I don't know," Eli said.

"So what's happening?" I said. "With you and Mom and Dad?"

Because they were talking and talking in the kitchen, and our mom was still crying and Dad sounded mad.

"Listen," Eli said. "Me and some friends here, we wanted to go to New York and help out, is all. Stuff like this happens, and you want to do something. You don't want to be one of those guys that just sits back on his ass. You remember when it's okay to say *ass*?"

"When it's a donkey or anything to do with Timmy Sperdle," I said. "I wish you were home."

"Danny, look, you're okay," Eli said. "They'll

28

figure out what happened and they'll take care of it. It's gonna be okay."

Then he said, "So you still in Hufflepuff?"

"Yeah," I said.

"That's cool," Eli said. "Hufflepuff sucks, but it doesn't suck as much as Slytherin. Those Slytherin kids are totally screwed."

"Our emblem is a stupid fat badger," I said. "Slytherin has a snake."

"Badgers are smarter than snakes," said Eli. "Snakes suck. When is it okay to say *suck*?"

"Vampires, vacuum cleaners, and anything to do with Timmy Sperdle," I said.

"Right," Eli said. "So you just go to bed, okay? I've got a clock right here that says it's past your pitiful eight-year-old bedtime. If you don't get your sleep, you'll grow up to be a midget. You'll have to stand on a stool to pee."

"I don't believe you," I said.

"Well, it's true," Eli said. "I swear and double-swear on a two-foot stack of Bibles. So get your short, skinny ass into bed. Now say 'Good night, Eli.'"

"Good night, Eli," I said.

"Good night, kid," Eli said.

Looking back, I think if my dad had just listened then, when Eli wanted to go help in New York, things would have turned out different. Maybe Eli wouldn't have joined the army if he'd gone and helped in New York.

I think if my dad had listened, we'd all be in a different parallel universe now, one with Eli still in it.

This was one reason I hated my dad.

CHAPTER 4

ARCHIMEDES (287–212 BCE)
Stabbed.

....

Daniel (E.) Anderson's Book of the Dead

Before I started keeping my Book of the Dead, all I knew about Archimedes was that thing about the bathtub, how he jumped out of it, naked as a jaybird, and went running through the streets hollering "Eureka!" He'd discovered that when you sit down in the tub, the water around you goes up, which seems to me more of a "duh" moment than anything else, but Walter says that scientifically it was a big deal.

Even so, you'd think he could have grabbed a towel.

Actually Archimedes wasn't as dumb as he sounds. When the Romans attacked his hometown on the island of Syracuse, Archimedes invented these great Roman-killing war machines. He built a giant iron claw that could yank Roman ships out of the water and a heat ray that used huge mirrors to make Roman ships burst into flames.

Some Greek archaeologist built a copy of Archimedes's heat ray a while back and burned up a rowboat with it, which I thought was pretty cool. For a while, Walter and I were thinking about trying to make one of our own to see if we could get Timmy Sperdle on his Jet Ski, but we never did.

Anyway, when the Romans finally conquered Syracuse, Marcellus, the Roman general-in-chief, gave orders that Archimedes was to be captured but not harmed. Walter says that in war everybody tries to grab the other side's brainpower, like after World War II when the Russians and the Americans scrambled to divvy up all the German rocket scientists, like Wernher von Braun.

But unfortunately not everybody listened to Marcellus. Some crap-for-brains soldier found Archimedes sitting there in the middle of the battle, working on a math problem, scratching diagrams of circles in the dust. And, just like that, he stabbed him to death. Archimedes's last words were supposed to have been "Don't disturb my circles."

I could see Walter dying like that. Getting so obsessed with what's going on inside his head that he doesn't notice that there's some thug the size of a refrigerator looming over him with a sword.

"Don't disturb my circles."

Walter would say that.

I didn't begin to know Walter until three years after Eli died, the summer after our freshman year, when we were both fourteen. That is, I knew who Walter *was*, because we'd been riding the same school bus back and forth twice a day since forever, but I didn't really *know* him, if you see what I mean.

Walter's is the bus stop after mine, so he's always gotten on after me on the way to school in the morning and gotten off before me on the way home in the afternoon. His is the stop at Cemetery Hill Road, which really isn't much of a hill or much of a road, or for that matter much of a cemetery either, just a bunch of old graves from before the Civil War, a lot of weeds, and a rusty iron fence that's falling down. The new cemetery, the one where Eli's buried, sort of butts up against it, but it's got a road of its own.

Nobody gets on the bus there but Walter, because Walter's is the only house on the road, which is a dead end. People used to tease Walter about that, and call him Zombie Boy and Wally the Living Dead, which was partly because of him living near the old cemetery and partly because of Walter himself.

Walter is tall and skinny, and when he's thinking, he has a habit of staring at nothing while his eyes flicker back and forth, back and forth, as if he's picking up signals from outer space. Walter says that thinking is the cerebral manipulation of information, so from the outside it doesn't look like anything much, but he's wrong there. From the outside that staring thing he does looks weird as hell.

Everybody always made fun of Walter, including me. I'm not proud of it, but that's the way it was. I've seen the same thing in Jim Pilcher's chickens, the way they'll gang up and peck at any chicken that's different. Jim keeps an eye out for that so that he can intervene before it goes too far and turns into a chicken bloodbath, but there wasn't anybody around then to keep an eye out for Walter. He'd hunch up his shoulders and turn his head as if he hadn't heard what we were saying, but we'd just keep pecking away.

By the time Walter got on the bus, I was always already there and sitting on the backseat with Peter Reilly and the other guys who hung around with Peter, like Mickey Roberts and Ryan Baker. Peter's friends are the popular kids, and the backseat is the best. For one thing, it's got the most legroom, and for another, it's the farthest from Earl Keever, the bus driver, who has a mean temper and chews Skoal Wintergreen tobacco, so he's always getting off the bus to spit. Everybody knew that the backseat was reserved for Peter and his friends, and it was a big deal if you got to sit there. It meant you were in.

Walter always sits in the very front seat, because Walter is about as far out as it's possible to get.

From where I sat, I could see the back of Walter's head, which stuck up above everybody else's because he's so tall, with his big poked-out ears and his really short haircut that his mother gave him at home that made him look like he'd backed into a pair of lawn clippers. He always wears white shirts buttoned all the way up to the very top button, the one that nobody normal ever buttons, and instead of carrying a backpack like the rest of us, he lugs around this funky old leather briefcase with buckles that looks like something some professor might carry in one of those movies set in a British boarding school.

Walter is terminally weird, but he's smart weird. In fact, he's the smartest person I've ever known, which explains why his only problem in the near future is going to be deciding whether he wants to go to Harvard or Stanford or MIT. When Walter was in third grade, he built a model of King Ludwig's castle in Bavaria with 11,265 sugar cubes, and in fourth grade, he made a *Tyrannosaurus rex* skeleton from chicken bones. It took three whole chickens, boiled.

Also he's read practically everything in the world, including stuff that nobody else would in a million years, like *The Iliad* by Homer and *On the Origin of*

Species by Charles Darwin and Stephen Hawking's *A Brief History of Time* and Plato's *Republic*.

Peter Reilly wouldn't leave Walter alone about reading Plato.

"Hey, Wally, you reading any more *Play-Doh*?" he'd yell.

And then we'd all chime in.

Peter is the captain of the hockey and soccer teams, and by our freshman year he'd had five serious girlfriends already, which was probably some kind of record. Freshman year it was Amanda Turner, who has long blond hair and boobs the size of watermelons and is the hottest girl in our class.

Peter's hair is practically white and cut sort of spiky, and he swaggers when he walks, very cool and laid-back, like Clint Eastwood in that movie where he says, "Go ahead, make my day." Peter has what they call leadership qualities, because people always somehow end up doing what he says. He was the person I always thought I'd want to be if I could be somebody other than me.

Not that I would have said so.

"In your dreams, Anderson," Peter would have said, and he'd have punched me in the arm, the way he does with friends.

Peter has a mean punch too. He works out on his brother Tony's Bowflex machine.

I'm on a couple of teams, but I'm not great at sports, not like Eli was. I don't do so great academically either, but I get by. Teachers like me, and the guys in my class think I'm a good sport, and the girls think I have a cute smile, so they call me sometimes on the phone.

To tell the truth, though, the year when I was fourteen, I could still take or leave girls. I liked girls all right, but not just one yet, like she was special.

I hadn't met Isabelle then.

CHAPTER 5

KING EDWARD V (1470–1483)
RICHARD, DUKE OF YORK (1473–1483)
(aka the Princes in the Tower)
Smothered.
....
Daniel (E.) Anderson's Book of the Dead

I didn't meet Isabelle first though. First I met the twins.

There aren't any twins in my Book of the Dead. The closest I've got are the two little Princes in the Tower, who were smothered to death when they were just kids by order of their wicked uncle, King Richard III. Their skeletons were found two hundred years later, stuffed under a staircase in the Tower of London.

On the other hand, after spending fifteen minutes or so with the twins, you start thinking maybe

King Richard had a point. I saw a picture of those princes once in some book, looking pretty harmless, with long golden curls and these little black velvet outfits. But looks can be deceptive. Maybe the little princes were real pains in the ass too.

Isabelle's family moved here just before school got out, sometime at the beginning of June. Her parents had taken a summer's lease on the old Sowers house, because Isabelle's father, who teaches history at some college, wanted a relaxing atmosphere in which to write a monograph about Oliver Cromwell and his pivotal role in the English Civil War, and Isabelle's mother, who is an artist, wanted to experience the rural countryside and paint interpretive pictures of fields and cows.

My dad said they'd been taken for a ride, and that if Harry Sowers weren't as tight as a duck's ass, he'd have bulldozed that damn place ten years ago and built some condos on top of the rubble and this time put in some insulation and modern plumbing. But I was just as glad he hadn't, because I always thought the old Sowers place was cool.

The Sowers house is the oldest house on our road. It's big and gray, with a porch with pillars all across the front and a funny little cupola up on top and a lot of huge tall windows with little panes of thick old wavy glass and about a million rooms. At the end of the driveway, there's a pair of stone gateposts where some past Sowers was thinking of putting something impressive in the way of statues, but whoever it was went broke before he did.

The Sowerses used to be rich way back when, but they lost all their money in 1929, when the stock market crashed and started the Great Depression. So the lions or griffins or Greek goddesses or whatever never got put on the gateposts, and ever since then, the house has been going downhill. Grandma O'Brian, my mother's mother, said that *her* mother remembered when there were dances and banquets at the Sowers house, and there used to be a French cook and maids in little ruffled aprons and caps and a chauffeur in a uniform with gold buttons and a cap with gold braid.

By the time Isabelle and her family moved in,

though, the yard was nothing but hay, and there were bats in the attic, and a lot of the wallpaper was brown with damp and peeling off the walls. But Isabelle didn't care. She liked the crown molding in the old Sowers dining room, and the claw-foot bathtubs, and the parlor with the gold peacocks on the walls.

The first I knew anybody was living there was when I was riding my bike past the house like I always did, and there were these two little kids running around in the hay that used to be a lawn with swords. Not real swords, but they looked pretty good for fakes. They had cross-shaped hilts trimmed with gold paint, and some kind of padded blades that were wrapped with duct tape.

"Have at thee, miscreant!" one of the kids screeched, lunging and slashing down a lot of hay. "Lay down thy arms and kneel! Know me for thy rightful lord!"

"No *way*!" the other one screeched back. "*I* am the rightful lord! Kneel down your stupid self! Or die!"

Then they both screamed "AARGH!" and started whacking each other.

So I stopped pedaling because in this neighborhood a hayfield sword battle with possible death involved is not something that you see every day.

They whacked each other back and forth for a while, yelling stuff like "Vile knave!" and "Cowardly churl!" and "Poltroon!" and then the first one turned and caught sight of me, and pointed a sword, and yelled "Hold! An enemy spy!"

Which gave the second one a chance to lay a pretty impressive whack across his back.

"OW! Lay off, Journey!" he said. "I said 'Hold!' Didn't you hear me say 'Hold'?"

"No," the second one said.

"Well, I did," the first one said, rubbing his back.

Then they both came up to the edge of the road, and I figured right then that they were twins because they looked almost exactly alike. They both had the same short dark hair, though the girl's was a little longer, and the same pointy chins and the same blue eyes with little flecks of gray and the same hard evil stare. The girl was wearing a Hello Kitty outfit that didn't go very well with the sword. The boy was wearing a T-shirt that said MWAHAHA!

The boy leveled his sword and pointed it at my chest.

"Cavalier or Roundhead?" he said.

"Oh, come on, Jasper," the girl said disgustedly. "Roundhead. Look at his hair. And his pants."

We all looked at my pants. As far as I could see, they were pretty much like everybody else's pants. Except Walter's, which are always too short due to his abnormal height and his tendency to wear his belt up around his chest.

"What's wrong with my pants?" I said.

"They're Roundhead pants," the girl said, staring at a point embarrassingly below my belt buckle.

"They're Levi's," I said. The staring was making me nervous. But when I looked, nothing was unzipped.

"It's just a game we play about people," the boy

explained. "We decide what kind of dinosaurs they'd be if they were dinosaurs or what kind of dog they'd be if they were dogs or what side they'd fight on in different wars. Like would they be Yankees or Confederates."

He gave the girl an accusing look.

"If Journey was a dinosaur, she'd be a velociraptor. You can tell by how she scorns fair play."

"I didn't hear you say 'Hold,'" the girl said.

Journey. *What kind of a name is that?* I thought. Like naming your kid Trip. Or GPS.

"If *Jasper* was a dinosaur, he'd be a stegosaurus," Journey said. "It had a brain the size of a Ping-Pong ball."

"What's a Cavalier?" I said hastily.

"The Cavaliers fought for the king in the English Civil War," Journey said. "They wore plumes in their hats and gave parties."

The twins, even though they were only nine, knew a lot about the English Civil War due to their father, the professor, and his monograph about Oliver

Cromwell, who won it. Isabelle told me later that the English Civil War was the world's most tedious topic of dinner conversation, but was good for the figure since after twenty minutes on the political implications of the Long Parliament, you'd do anything to get away from the table, even give up banana cream pie for dessert.

"The Roundheads fought with Oliver Cromwell against the king," Jasper said. "They were Puritans."

"The Roundheads had stupid haircuts and never had any fun," Journey said. "*Jasper* would have been a Roundhead."

"The Cavaliers all ended up exiled in France or with their heads chopped off," Jasper said. "Have you ever been to France?"

"No," I said.

"*Je parle français*," Journey said. "That means 'I speak French' in French. I have an unusual aptitude for languages."

"No, you don't," Jasper said.

"So you'd be a Roundhead," Journey continued, still disturbingly eyeing my pants, "because your hair is short and you have plain clothes and stuff. If you were a Cavalier, you'd be fancier. Like you'd have an earring."

She gave Jasper a dirty look and whacked some hay viciously with her sword.

"And I do so speak French."

"If Journey was a mechanical device," Jasper said, "she'd be a Kalashnikov automatic rifle."

He glared at Journey.

"And you don't."

These kids should be in an institution, I thought. The kind with padded walls where they don't let you use anything but plastic knives and forks.

"We play Cavaliers and Roundheads all the time," Journey said. "Except when we're doing the Crusaders and the Saracens or Attila the Hun and the barbarian hordes. When we do the Crusaders, Jasper is always Richard the Lionheart. He doesn't like being a Saracen because then he has to have a harem full of wives. Would you want to have a harem full of wives?"

"No," I said feelingly. I remembered what Peter

Reilly went through with his first five serious girl-friends.

"Nobody would," Jasper said to Journey. "I told you."

"If Jasper was a blanket," Journey said, "he would be a cold wet blanket."

"So where did you move here from?" I said.

"Jasper says he is a member of an alien race," Journey said. "He is from a galaxy far far away and is only here observing this planet until the mother ship comes to take him home."

It made me nervous how much sense that made to me.

"But Isabelle says that's crap," Journey said cheerfully.

Which was the first time I heard Isabelle's name.

I said, "Who's Isabelle?"

CHAPTER 6

ISADORA DUNCAN (1877–1927)
Died of a broken neck.

....

Daniel (E.) Anderson's Book of the Dead

Here's something Isadora Duncan once said: "Don't let them tame you."

Isadora was a dancer, but she hated classical ballet. Instead she invented modern dance, which involved barefoot people wearing togas and pretending to be the wind. When she wasn't wearing her toga, she wore long flowing silk scarves.

She was wearing one of those scarves in 1927 when she leaped into a car, made a grand gesture, and cried, "Good-bye, my friends, I am off to glory!" When the car started up, the scarf somehow got tangled up in the wheel, yanked tight, and broke her neck.

I could see Isabelle dying like that. Wild and beautiful and kind of crazy, but untamed. And making a grand gesture. That's something Isabelle would do.

By the time I met Isabelle, it was the second week in June and school was just out for the summer. The lilacs had come and gone by then, the blackflies had come and stayed, and the temperature had gone so fast from cool to hot that Corrigan's Hardware Store had to scramble, setting out window screens and ice-cube trays and fans.

On the last day of school we all got rowdy on the back seat of the bus on the way home, yelling and laughing and shoving each other around. Partly it was because it was just a great day outside and there was a whole summer in front of us, and partly, at least in my case, it was because I knew that for two whole months now I wouldn't have to worry about my untapped potential and my crappy grades and how disgusted my dad was going to be when I got like a 10 on the PSAT. So we were whooping and hollering like idiots, and punching each other in the arm, especially Peter Reilly with his Bowflex biceps.

When Walter got off the bus at Cemetery Hill Road, we yanked the window down and started throwing Ryan Baker's gourmet jelly beans at him, pinging them off his shoulders and the back of his head, the ones with flavors nobody liked, like mango and grape jelly. Walter didn't even look up, just hunched over and trudged off down the road, lugging his funky briefcase.

Peter Reilly yelled after him, "Hey, Wally! What are you going to do this summer? Read *Play-Doh*?" and Mickey Roberts yelled, "Say hi to the Living Dead!" and all the rest of us went, "Woo-oo-oo-oo!" like horror-movie noises, but Walter didn't so much as turn around. I thought for a minute how he looked sad and lonely there, scuffing along in the dust where the county hadn't come out yet to put calcium chloride down on the dirt road, but then Ryan Baker got up in the aisle and started playing air guitar and Earl Keever bellowed at him to set his scrawny rump back down, and I didn't think about Walter anymore.

Final exams had been pretty excruciating, though a bright spot was that we're allowed to wear anything we want within reason to school in exam week, and Amanda Turner showed up in a halter top and a pair of little shorts that barely covered her rear end. Peter Reilly said at lunch that it was her fault if he flunked ninth grade because every time he looked up from thinking about algebra or American history, there was that halter top across the aisle and then everything would go right out of his head. Peter said he'd heard somewhere that men think about sex every ten seconds, but he figured Amanda in that halter top brought it down to five.

The teachers must have realized this too, because Amanda got called to the office, and when she came back, she was covered up from neck to knees in one of those baggy white coats from the chemistry lab.

I ended up with one B, four C's, and one A, which was in physical education, which yet again dashed my dad's hopes of me ever making something of myself someday. I knew he looked at my report cards and thought what a waste I was, and how Eli could have been out of medical school by now, with a profession and a title. That's what Eli was going to be, a doctor. Except he decided to go to Iraq and be a combat medic first.

"Yeah," my dad said, looking at my card like it was an HIV-positive blood test. "You know, I don't think Eli ever got less than a B in high school, and he only got one of those."

He dropped my report card on the coffee table.

"It was in German," he said. "He got a B in German. From that bald guy who didn't like him. The one who looked like a Nazi."

"Mr. Trossel," I said.

"Those A's in phys ed, I read they don't mean anything when it comes to getting into college," my dad said. "Colleges want the kids to play some sport, sure, but when they look at a GPA, all they want is the academics. The academics, that's what counts."

By which time I felt lower than a worm's belly. He

never said I was a failure straight out, but it didn't take a genius to see what he was thinking. Like those canaries that can sense poisonous gases in coal mines, I could sense the condemnation in the air.

So that afternoon I took my bike out and went for a ride.

Walter says the only way to solve problems is to think them through in logical sequence, but I know that if you go far enough and fast enough on a bike, you can leave them all behind, at least for a while. I used to pedal and pedal until the muscles in the calves of my legs burned and my eyes teared up from wind, and then I'd feel things sort of loosen up inside, like they didn't matter so much anymore. I always thought that maybe Lance Armstrong is such a great racer because he had a crappy dad and this terrible cancer and he knew what it was like to have problems to outrun.

I had two or three different favorite rides. One went up over the top of Turkey Hill, and that was the hardest, because it's really steep, and when I first started riding there, I used to have to stop in the middle and get off and push my bike for a while. It was always worth it though, because coming back down was wild, as good as a roller-coaster ride, with the bike going about a hundred miles an hour and me feeling like I wasn't on earth at all but was some kind of supermagic creature flying on the wind. Then the road levels out past the Monroe place and through the back end of the Pilcher property, where Jim has his blue-potato farm, and then out to the Fairfield Road and back home.

Or I'd ride out past the old Sowers place and take a left onto Scrubgrass Creek Road, which goes back through the woods and across this rickety little bridge over the creek. That was prettier, with dogwood and crab-apple flowers in the springtime, and all the leaves red and yellow in the fall, and it smelled better too. The Monroes have pigs, and those can be pretty repulsive if the wind is blowing the wrong way.

Anyway, that afternoon I rode out past the old Sowers house. Already it was looking different, now that it was being lived in again. There was a Volvo parked in the driveway, and furniture on the porch, and a hanging basket with a pink geranium. A lot of the hay had been cut down too, to make what was starting to look like a lawn.

Then I saw that right in the middle of the lawn was this girl lying flat on her back with her arms stretched out and her eyes closed, and next to her, flat out too, were the sword-fighting twins. Right off I thought of a horrible murder scene like in *CSI*, with bodies scattered around. I could imagine them all outlined in chalk, with one of those yellow-tape things that the police put up that says DO NOT CROSS THIS LINE.

But then the twins jumped up and came running over. Jasper was wearing a purple T-shirt that said I AM THE EVIL TWIN. Journey was wearing a purple leotard and one of those little ballet skirts and a pair of purple Crocs. It wasn't often that I saw so much short purple all in one place.

"What are you two supposed to be?" I said. "Grapes?"

Journey shot me a look that said that if I was a fruit, I'd be a poison apple.

"Purple is our favorite color," said Jasper. "People who like purple are witty and sensitive."

"I used to like pink," Journey said. "But Isabelle says that pink is a color stereotype. You know, like blue is for boys and pink is for girls. If Isabelle ever has a baby boy, she's going to dress him in pink because she thinks color stereotypes are stupid."

I thought that if she really carried through with that, she'd also better get the kid a set of brass knuckles and a crash course in karate.

"Right now we're listening to the earth hum," Journey said. "It's Isabelle's idea. She read about it in *Scientific American.* She read that the earth hums all the time like a giant bumblebee."

"Like this," Jasper said, making a repulsive noise through his nose.

Then Isabelle sat up and I forgot about the twins.

What I knew by then about Isabelle, due to the twins' having no sense of privacy or discretion, was that she was fifteen and went to some fancy school for the arts back home, which was in New York City, where she had a boyfriend named Simon Dewitt

Paxton, who was presently spending a multicultur-ally enriching summer living with a family in France. I also knew that if she were a bird, she'd be a vicious parrot; that when the twins were three, she'd talked them into eating a bar of Ivory soap; and that she dis-approved of cowboy hats.

What I didn't know, because the twins hadn't bothered to say in spite of the fact that they have the verbal version of diarrhea, was that she was beauti-ful. *Beautiful* was not a word I usually used about girls, but it was the only word for Isabelle.

Walter says that we are attracted to potential mates because of large differences in our major histocompatibility complexes, which are a bunch of genes that have something to do with making us immune to disease. Attraction is purely genetic and instinctive, Walter says, though I can tell you that if Walter does not learn to shut up about this, he will never have a potential mate.

Anyway, I did not think about disease genes right then. What I thought about was how I'd never seen anybody as beautiful as Isabelle. And how Isabelle made Amanda Turner and her halter tops look too bright and loud, like those plastic dolls you win for throwing baseballs at ducks at the Fairfield County Agricultural Fair. She had straight, silky dark hair and skin like cream and these blue, blue eyes, the color the sky gets on a really perfect October afternoon. Everything about her was slim and crisp and elegant. If you've ever known a truly beautiful girl, you'll know what I mean, and if you haven't, I can't explain. It was just everything that Isabelle was.

That day she had on a white skirt and an old soft blue shirt and she wasn't wearing any shoes. And she had this beautiful smile that just sparkled at you, that made you feel special, as if you were the person she'd been most hoping to see.

And there I was, all sweaty from riding my bicycle, and a pimple starting on my nose, and I probably smelled.

"You must be Danny," Isabelle said.

She patted the grass next to her and said, "Come

listen with us," and where I would ordinarily have thought about the red ants and deer ticks and Lyme disease, right then I didn't. For a chance to be next to Isabelle, I would have laid down on a bed of nails in a crocodile swamp.

"It's a very low-pitched hum, so you have to be quiet," Isabelle said. "It's like a giant heartbeat. The heart of the planet."

"Babies inside their mother can hear their mother's heart," said Journey. "They can hear their mother reading to them too. When Jasper and I were inside, our mother used to read to us, which is why we are so intelligent. She read us poetry and philosophy and *Winnie-the-Pooh*."

"Hush," Isabelle said.

"I don't hear anything," Jasper said, squirming.

"That's because you're talking," Isabelle said. "Close your eyes and hold your breath and listen. Concentrate."

So we all closed our eyes and held our breath and listened, though I couldn't concentrate very well, being so close to Isabelle. I hoped right then that

Simon Dewitt Paxton would never come back from France. I'd read somewhere that there were wolves in France. Maybe he'd get eaten by wolves. Or run over by a taxi on the Champs Elysées, which Walter told me later was a lot more likely.

Then for a minute I thought I could hear something deep, deep down in the ground, like a huge old string bass with strings as big around as your arm. *Thrum.*

"Hey!" I said. "I think I hear it."

Walter says the earth really does hum but that nobody can possibly hear it because it's a sound way too low for human ears. It's somehow caused by changes in planetary air pressure. We're lucky we can't hear it, Walter says, because it's a really boring hum. It's the cosmic hum equivalent of "Ninety-nine Bottles of Beer on the Wall."

Isabelle reached over and put a hand on my arm and squeezed.

Thrum. Thrum. Thrum.

Of course it could just have been the blood beating in my ears, because what with Isabelle right next to me, and now with her hand on my arm, my heart was going about a million miles a minute.

Journey said, "I don't hear any hum."

"You have to be *quiet*," Isabelle said. "You have to feel the earth around you and be one with the grass and the ground and the rocks."

The twins were quiet for maybe six seconds.

"This is boring," Journey said.

"If Journey was a hum," Jasper said, "she would be a high whiny hum like a malaria mosquito."

Isabelle took her hand off my arm and sat up.

"You don't deserve to live on this planet," she said. "Neither of you."

"I am from a more interesting planet than this," Jasper said. "On my planet there is purple light and very little gravity."

"Great," Isabelle said. "Scram. Go out behind the barn and watch for the mother ship."

The twins took off in a flash of purple, giving us more poison-apple looks.

Isabelle pulled her skirt up above her knees and stretched out her legs in the sun. She had great legs, and I kept trying not to stare at them. It was hard with Isabelle to find a place not to stare at.

"My mother took fertility drugs trying to get pregnant with them—can you imagine?" Isabelle said. "And then she had to stay in bed for six months with her feet up. And look what came of it."

I thought that sounded nice, actually, that Isabelle's mother had gone to so much trouble to have a baby. My uncle Al once let slip after a couple of gin and tonics at a family-reunion picnic that I'm only here because of a disastrous failure in a contraceptive device.

"When they were babies, every time I went near them, they'd scream," Isabelle said. "I think they did it on purpose. They were diabolical. I was always getting blamed for abusing them."

"My brother said the first thing I did when I came home from the hospital was puke on his Pittsburgh Penguins T-shirt," I said. "He always said it was the start of a beautiful relationship. It was years before I figured out he was being sarcastic."

"I heard your brother died in the war," Isabelle said.

Immediately I had a whole lot of shameful thoughts. First I thought that maybe Isabelle would feel sorry for me, knowing I was bereaved, since girls are often softhearted that way, and that maybe she would want to comfort me in my bereavement and we could go for long walks on Scrubgrass Creek Road where the little bridge is and we could talk and hold hands. I thought that maybe it made me interesting, being bereaved, and I started trying to look bereaved while sneakily staring at Isabelle's legs at the same time. Then I thought what a disgusting creep I was to think thoughts like that.

What I said (brilliant, Danny) was, "Yeah."

"It must be glorious, in a way," Isabelle said. "To be brave enough to sacrifice your life for what you believe in. Like Sydney Carton in *A Tale of Two Cities*, going to the guillotine in place of his friend Charles, who was married to the woman Sydney was in love with. He gave up his life for her happiness. His last words were, 'It is a far, far better thing that I do, than I have ever done.' Don't you think that's romantic?"

Romantic was always one of Isabelle's words.

I remembered when Eli was reading *A Tale of Two Cities* for an English-lit class he took in college. He said it sucked except for the creepy old lady who sat there knitting and watching the chopped-off heads fall into baskets.

Then I thought how if Sydney Carton had had the sense God gave a chicken, he would have let Charles go to the guillotine, like he was supposed to, in which case Sydney could have lived happily ever after and gotten the girl. That's what I would have done if I'd been Sydney. But I couldn't say that to Isabelle.

"I don't know that he thought it was glorious," I said. "He was all upset about Nine Eleven. He was angry that anybody would kill innocent people like that."

"Nine Eleven was so terrible," Isabelle said. "A girl in my class, her dad got killed in one of the towers. And I used to have nightmares about those people jumping with their hair on fire. For a long time I wrote only very dark poems."

We were quiet while Isabelle thought about dark poems.

"Let's not talk about it," she said. "Let's talk about something else. Tell me about you."

So I started telling her about where I went to school and what teams I was on, but she stopped me somewhere in the middle of junior-varsity soccer.

"No, darling, that's what you *do*," she said. "That's not who you *are*. Tell me who you *are*. What do you love? What do you hate? Whom do you admire? If you could be a month of the year, what month would you be?"

That pretty much stopped me cold, so Isabelle talked instead.

If Isabelle could be a month, she'd be July, because of fireworks and lightning and thunderstorms.

Things she loves are peppermint ice cream, silver earrings, Johann Sebastian Bach, full moons, tigers, amethysts, merry-go-rounds, and Emily Dickinson; and things she hates are fast food, Barney the purple dinosaur, shopping malls, tattoos, hair spray, paper plates, Britney Spears, and the oil-based economy.

People she admires are Buddha, Jesus, Amelia Earhart, and Langston Hughes, who quit Columbia University and got a job on a boat to Europe and threw all his textbooks into the sea because he wanted to write poems.

I didn't get the textbook thing.

"You know those books cost two hundred bucks a pop?" I said.

"It was a grand romantic gesture," Isabelle said.

"Well, sure," I said hastily, though to tell the truth I didn't get it. Eli always said you could get good money for those books from the textbook exchange. I thought how that would maybe have bought Langston Hughes a lot of sandwiches and ballpoint pens.

"I'm going to write someday," Isabelle said. "I already am writing, actually. But not on a computer. That always seems soulless, don't you think? To share all your feelings with a machine?"

"Uh," I said.

"If I could, I'd write in gold ink with a swan's quill," Isabelle said. "Virginia Woolf always wrote in purple. And Pablo Neruda wrote in green."

"Green is nice," I said. Dumb. I never could keep up with Isabelle.

But the thing was, when she told you things like that, you felt special, like she was sharing something private just with you. Listening to Isabelle made me feel like I was standing in a sort of golden spotlight all the time.

My mom missed Eli so much that I used to feel like I was invisible. After Eli died, it was as if she couldn't see real people anymore. She could only see ghosts. She'd stop all the time in the middle of doing something and just stand there staring at nothing, and then she'd go up to her room and shut the door. Sometimes at night I'd hear her walking around downstairs, just walking back and forth for hours, going from room to room in the dark.

For a while I used to go around writing my name on things. DANNY, I'd write, over and over. On my arm, on my sneakers, on the wall in my bedroom, inside my desk at school. DANNY, in permanent black ink. I think it was my way of reminding myself that I was still there.

With Isabelle, I felt real. Everything sparkled with Isabelle. With Isabelle, I didn't want to be Peter Reilly. I wanted to be me.

I guess that was why I was in love with her.

I guess that's why in a way I still am.

CHAPTER 7

JENNIE WADE (1843–1863)
Shot at the Battle of Gettysburg.
....
Daniel (E.) Anderson's Book of the Dead

In the entire three days of the Battle of Gettysburg, only one civilian got killed. Her name was Jennie Wade, and she was in the kitchen kneading bread dough when a bullet came through the door and went right into her heart. She dropped dead on the kitchen floor, becoming what the U.S. Army calls collateral damage.

Collateral damage is someone you kill by mistake when you're really trying to kill somebody else. Though as it turns out there are lots of ways of killing people that don't involve actual death. Like how Eli's death did in my mom and dad.

My parents never got over Eli dying. My dad, who was never an easy person to live with, became pure hell. And my mom just sort of curled in on herself and shriveled up. She used to be bright and funny, and she had a lot of friends and a job teaching kindergarten at the elementary school in Fairfield. But she quit that after Eli died. After Eli died, she just stayed home.

The first year after Eli died, I used to do stuff all the time to try to make her feel better. Sometimes I'd bring her presents, like the napkin holder with her name on it that I made in the 3-D project part of Visual Arts class. Or I'd come home after school and make her a cup of Lipton tea and arrange Fig Newtons in circles on a plate, like in fancy restaurants, and I'd take them up to the bedroom where she spent a lot of time lying on the bed with the shades pulled down.

She'd say, "Just put it there on the table, Danny," and I could tell by the way she said it that she wasn't going to eat those cookies.

Much later, when I told Isabelle about it, she said

71

that maybe the Fig Newtons were a mistake, because everyone knows that real comfort food has chocolate in it. But I think that for my mom there wasn't any comfort food.

Her heart was broken. For a long time I thought that she was going to die too.

Walter says it really is possible to die of a broken heart. Though it's not really a break, Walter says, but more of a pop after part of your heart blows up like a balloon. Great emotional stress, like after someone dies, messes up the heart muscles until they go all weak and start to bulge, and if they bulge too much, you die. Officially this is a condition called takotsubo cardiomyopathy, which nobody on earth can pronounce except Japanese fishermen, medical doctors, and Walter. The *takotsubo* part is the Japanese word for "octopus trap." Japanese octopus traps are these big roundish pots, the same shape that a broken heart takes on before it blows.

At which point Walter got sidetracked onto octopuses and how nobody has any business trapping them because they're as smart as dogs, so eating an octopus is like chowing down on Man's Best Friend. Walter's favorite animal is the octopus.

Dogs can die of broken hearts. When old Mr. Pilcher, Jim Pilcher's granddad, died, his dog, Bernie, just lay down and died too. When they all got back from the funeral, Jim said, there was Bernie, all cold and stiff on the floor, with his head on old Mr. Pilcher's needlepoint carpet slippers, the ones he used to chew.

When we got the news about Eli, that was one thing I thought of — that I was glad he didn't have a dog. Or, I guess, an octopus, though back then I didn't know how smart they were.

Isabelle thought it would be romantic to die of a broken heart, like Romeo and Juliet, though Walter says that in their case death was helped along by poison, stupidity, and a failure to communicate.

"If Simon died, I would simply waste away," Isabelle said.

We were all sitting under one of the big old trees

on the Sowers lawn because it was shady and there was a little breeze. Isabelle was wearing a denim skirt and a shirt with little puffed sleeves, embroidered all over with flowers and birds. She leaned back against the tree trunk and got a sort of dreamy, faraway look.

"I would lie on a brocade sofa wearing a long white nightgown with little pearl buttons, and a white lace shawl over my knees, and I would grow thinner and frailer and paler, and finally, when the last leaf fell, my spirit would go with it."

Simon, aka Simon Dewitt Paxton, was now pigging out on chocolate éclairs in France. Isabelle wore a gold chain around her neck with a little gold pendant in the shape of half a heart, and Simon had a matching gold chain with the other heart half, which showed that they were pledged to each other.

The only good thing I knew about Simon was that the twins called him Dewittless.

"When the last leaf falls, can I have your iPod?" Journey said. "And your turquoise bracelet?"

"If Journey died, *I* wouldn't waste away," Jasper

said. "I would get to sleep in the top bunk whenever we visit Uncle Paul. And I would get a companion dog."

"If Jasper died, I would get *two* companion dogs," Journey said.

I must have looked kind of funny then, because Isabelle stopped looking dreamy and told them to shut up, and for a while after that, we didn't talk about broken hearts or dying anymore.

How the army deals with dying is with acronyms.

The worst job in the army must be CNO, which stands for Casualty Notification Officer. The CNO is the person who goes around telling people that somebody in their family has just become a KIA, which means Killed in Action. Our CNO was named Captain Eula Bates, and her teammate was a sergeant twice her size with practically no hair.

Everybody gets told about their KIA the same way. There's a standard speech.

"The secretary of defense has asked me to express

his deep regret that your son Eli was killed in action in Iraq when his vehicle encountered a roadside bomb. The secretary extends his deepest sympathy to you and your family in your tragic loss."

"Oh, Jesus," my father said. "Oh, Jesus." Sort of gasping for air, as if somebody had punched him in the stomach.

My mother said, "Oh, God, no," and just sat down on the chair in the hall as if her legs had lost their bones. Her arms were clutched tight across her middle, and her face had gone so white and pinched up that you could see what she'd look like when she was really old.

"A Casualty Assistance Officer will be in touch to help you with further details," Captain Bates said.

Spelling it out for us, because the army just says *CAO*.

Then she and the sergeant drove away in their van, leaving us to begin our LWE. Life Without Eli.

The thing about death is that it takes a while before you realize that it's never going to go away.

That sounds stupid, but it's true. For months after we knew Eli was dead, I'd find myself thinking about the things we'd do when he came home or hearing a joke he'd like, or there'd be something I'd want to tell him. Then I'd remember all over again.

I'd think how now on every Thanksgiving, Eli's chair would be empty and he wouldn't be there to say grace. Eli always said these awful graces.

He'd say, "Dear God, in your infinite wisdom, please protect your humble servants from the unspeakable turkey tetrazzini we were forced to eat last year in a misguided attempt by my mother, thy handmaiden, to use up thy leftovers," or "Dear Lord, grant me the serenity to accept the things I cannot change, the courage to change the things I cannot accept, and the cleverness to make that asshole Timmy Sperdle eat dirt, since he is one of thy worst mistakes."

Then my mom would threaten to bean him with the gravy ladle.

I'd think how now there'd be nothing for him

under the Christmas tree and how he wouldn't be here cheering for me when I graduated from high school, like he'd promised, or be around to take me out to Rudy's Beverage Bar & Barbecue Grill for my first legal beer. We'd already had one Christmas without Eli, but that wasn't so bad, because we figured next year he'd be back home. We sent him a package with these gingerbread men that my mom and I decorated to look like little soldiers, and on Christmas morning Eli called us — on the computer, so that we could see him — though he couldn't talk for very long.

Afterward my mom cried.

"He looked so tired and thin," she said. "Didn't you think he looked tired and thin?"

"For God's sake, Ellen," my dad said. "Of course he's tired and thin. They're all tired and thin."

I knew what she meant, though. He looked different. Older.

I had a calendar that Eli got me before he left. I'd cross off every day with an *X*, waiting for the big circled day at the end, which was when his tour of duty was up and he'd be coming home. That was the best part of that last Christmas. X-ing off another day until Eli came home.

When I was a little kid, Eli's being older used to really piss me off. I remember throwing a tantrum when I was maybe five or six. I can't remember what set me off—I wanted to stay up past seven thirty or see some movie that wasn't G-rated with animated singing mice or something—but I was mad enough to pop a gasket.

"Why do you always have to be older than me?" I yelled. Stamping around in my choo-choo train pajamas because Eli got to do everything and he could stay up late and drive a car and stay home by himself without a babysitter, and I never got to do anything I wanted to do, ever. I was steamed.

Eli grabbed me by my choo-choo collar and said I'd grow up eventually unless I kept screeching, which would probably permanently freeze my vocal cords, so that I'd always talk like a girl, and I might as well face it that his being older was just the way it was.

"Live with it, kid. When you're eighty, I'll be ninety-two," he said. "I'll be old and irascible, and if you give me any of your pitiful underage eighty-year-old lip, I'll whack your butt with my cane."

Then he tickled me until I got the hiccups, and then we watched *The Lion King*.

We never thought then that when I was eighty, Eli would still be twenty-two.

CHAPTER 8

JIM MORRISON (1943–1971)
Died of a drug overdose.
....
Daniel (E.) Anderson's Book of the Dead

Most of the guys I hung around with had jobs that summer. Peter Reilly was using all his Bowflex biceps to haul cement blocks and boards for his dad and his brother Tony, who ran the family construction business. Mickey Roberts was doing dishes at the pizza parlor, which included getting a twelve-inch pepperoni-and-mushroom pizza every night for free, which Mickey didn't need, having inherited the Roberts family tendency for flab, and Ryan Baker was pumping gas and changing tires at his uncle Bug's garage.

All Ryan's uncles have weird nicknames. Bug got his name from once eating a Japanese beetle on a dare. His uncle Rat, who works at Rudy's Beverage Bar & Barbecue Grill, is called Rat because when he was about ten, he lost a little piece of his thumb by getting it caught in a rat trap, and his uncle Chop is named for Precious Pork Chop, which is what his mom used to call him when he was a fat little baby, though when Ryan told me that, he said never to mention it in front of Uncle Chop unless I wanted to lose my front teeth.

Ryan's father, who must have wised up fast about the nickname thing, refuses to answer to anything but George.

My dad didn't want me to get a job. He wanted me to spend the summer in remedial school, cranking up my math scores and improving my reading comprehension and study skills, which basically he did not think it possible for me to do.

"I can't force you to make an effort, Daniel," my dad said.

The "Daniel" being a bad signal, since I had learned in Eli's Education Days that nothing good comes of an authority figure using your full name.

"But I'd like you to realize that unless you start thinking seriously about the future, you're not going to have much of one. Look at Jim Pilcher."

Jim Pilcher was Eli's best friend in high school, and my dad always brought him up after viewing my pitiful report cards.

My dad thinks Jim pretty much screwed up his life, because by now, instead of hoeing potatoes, he should be working for NASA, designing space colonies, or working for some gaming company inventing something like *Half-Life II* and making a gazillion dollars. Jim had an engineering scholarship to the state university, but he got hung up on this girl who dumped him, and then he got burned out on drugs and then he dropped out of college in the middle of his sophomore year. Then he was in rehabilitation for a while, and later his grandfather, old Mr. Pilcher, gave him a piece of land and he started an organic farm.

My dad says that, what with the drugs and all, Jim is now one taco short of a combination platter. Though sometimes he says "two bears short of a picnic."

"If I'm so dumb, more school would just be a stupid waste of money," I said. "Anyway, there's nothing wrong with Jim. *Eli* liked Jim."

"Don't take that tone with me, young man," my dad said. "Do you *want* to spend your life flipping burgers? You want to be one of those guys that says, 'Want fries with that?' Well, that's where you're headed if you don't watch your step. This is for your own good."

On one of Eli's Education Days, I'd learned that "This is for your own good" is one of the four crucial Bullshit Alert Phrases, along with "You'll just have to take my word for it," "This hurts me more than it hurts you," and "You kids these days don't know when you have it easy." Eli always said there should be some sort of inoculation for bullshit, like for measles and chicken pox.

"That's bullshit," I said.

"That's enough of that lip," my dad said. "And let me tell you something else, Daniel. That book of dead people you keep messing with isn't doing you any good either. It's not normal, sitting up in that room and collecting dead people like they were stamps. You think it's good to be mooning around about death all the time? The best thing you could do for yourself right now is to throw that damn book in the trash."

"Everybody in this damn house moons around about death all the time," I said. "I'm not the one you should be calling sick. Why don't you go talk to Mom about being sick? She doesn't even talk to anybody anymore. Don't you even care that she doesn't talk to anybody anymore?"

"You don't know anything about it, Daniel," my dad said.

And he turned on his heel and went out to the kitchen to get a beer.

"Shut up," I said, but only after he was out of the room.

Sometimes I really hated my dad.

Anyway, before he had a chance to pay the nonrefundable tuition fee to his saving-me-from-burgers remedial school, I talked Jim Pilcher into hiring me to work at the blue-potato farm.

Back when Jim was all messed up and in rehab, Eli used to go see him a lot. I know because Eli and my dad had a fight about it.

I was under the dining-room table during the fight, playing with my Lego pirate ship, and the table-cloth was hanging down, so it was like a secret hide-out. I used to spend a lot of time under that table. Also that pirate ship was cool. It had all these pirates with cutlasses, and a captain pirate with an eye patch and a parrot on his shoulder. I really loved that little parrot.

I was in the middle of burying a chest of plastic treasure under a plastic palm tree on a plastic island when I heard my dad say, "Eli, you've got to quit this crap. What the hell are you thinking? Cutting out of college to run over there all the time? Jesus, you got a *warning.* There was a letter sent here by some *dean.* What is this? Are you crazy?"

There were creaky noises that were from my dad walking back and forth across the floor like he does when he's telling you how screwed up you are. The way the floorboards squeak in our front room is as good as a burglar alarm. At least that's what my parents always said whenever I wanted a dog.

"Jim's my best friend, Dad," Eli said.

"Well, that kind of best friend doesn't do you a single lick of good," my dad said. "People judge you by your friends. Right now what you've got to do is get good grades, make good connections, and keep that scholarship. That's what you've got to do, Eli. Jim's not your responsibility. Jim's already getting all the help he needs."

"I'm not going to lose my scholarship," Eli said.

"You'd better not," my dad said. "That's not a cheap school you're at, Eli. Your mother and I can't pay for that school. So I don't want to hear any more about you cutting class. Not for Jim. He's screwed up his life, and that's his business, but I'm not about to watch you screw up yours. Do you hear me, Eli?"

"Yeah, I hear you," Eli said.

"Good," my dad said.

After my dad was gone, Eli came over to the table and kicked the tablecloth.

"You in there, Dan?" he said.

I wasn't sure I wanted to be, but I said I guessed I was.

Eli hunkered down, pulled up the tablecloth, and poked his head underneath.

"You hear all that?"

"Yeah," I said.

"I don't know what you've got for a bunch of little runt drip-nose friends," Eli said. "But if you ever get a real friend, you don't wimp out when there's trouble or he's going through a bad patch and acting like a dick. You got that, Danny?"

He sounded pissed, but not at me. Also really serious.

"Dad's mad," I said. "That's a hink-pink."

"No shit, nitwit," Eli said. "That's a hinky-pinky. And when is it okay to say *shit*?"

"Never in front of Mom or Aunt Wendy and always when it has something to do with Timmy Sperdle," I said.

"You got it, Captain Kidd," Eli said. "Go back to your pieces of eight."

He dropped the tablecloth and I heard his feet going, fast and angry, across the creaky floor, and then the front door slammed.

My dad still doesn't like Jim.

Jim has long hair in a ponytail, and he wears Birkenstock sandals, and he votes for left-wing causes that my dad says would send the country straight to hell in a handcart if Congress ever got its act together and passed a bill. Also Jim's farm isn't like normal farms, which my dad says is a sign of something wrong right there.

Not only does Jim not use chemicals, but he grows all these crops that come in funny colors, like blue potatoes and white pumpkins and black carrots, or in weird shapes, like rattlesnake beans, that coil up like snakes, and these big warty Hubbard squashes that, if you didn't know they were vegetables, look like something you ought to kill quick with a baseball bat before it eats your house pets. The farm's name is the Blue Potato, which is also weird, because most farms around here, if they have names at all, are called things like Monroe's Pigs.

"I need help weeding and watering and hauling manure and picking the bugs off stuff and hoeing the blue potatoes," Jim said. "If the help could do all that without stomping on anything or killing anything through neglect, that would be a plus. You think you can handle it?"

"I think so," I said. "Sure."

"And you'll have to drink these things that Emma'll make for you," Jim said. "They're all pure vitamins and if you choke one down every day, you'll live to be a hundred and ten with all your own teeth and hair and your sex drive intact. So just do it, man, and don't hurt her feelings. Consider it part of the job."

I said that sounded okay too, though at the time I hadn't yet come face-to-face with Emma's black-carrot smoothies.

Emma is Jim's live-in girlfriend, and she's another thing my dad doesn't like about Jim.

Emma comes from River City, which isn't a city but just the name people give to the bad part of town, that's all trailers and ratty little falling-down houses with junk cars in the yard. Peter Reilly and I went over there on our bikes once or twice, just to see what it was like, and Peter said that all the guys hanging out were drug dealers, and there was one house with pink Christmas-tree lights that Peter said was full of whores.

He told me to go up and knock on the door, and I said I'd go if he'd go first, and he said I should go because he'd already done it lots of times, and I said, "That's bullshit, O'Reilly," and while we were fighting about it and Peter was punching my arm, some lady came out on the porch and yelled at us to get off her front lawn. She didn't look like a whore. She looked like somebody's grandmother.

Peter's brother, Tony, says all the girls from River City are whores. So I figured Emma would be really hot, with tight rhinestone T-shirts and high-heeled shoes and lots of red lipstick and puffy platinum-blond hair.

But as it turned out, Emma isn't like that at all. Actually, Emma isn't even exactly pretty. She has this flat, round face spattered all over with freckles, and a lot of reddish frizzy hair, and she wears these baggy jeans. The first thing I thought when I saw her was that Jim really had cooked part of his brain, like in that old fried-egg ad that used to be on TV. Where they had this egg sizzling in a frying pan and a voice-over that said, really ominously, *This is your brain on drugs.*

Emma made me come into the kitchen and sit down, and she gave me some cookies made out of flax or something that people don't normally make cookies out of. They tasted funny, but I ate them anyway to be polite.

"They're my own recipe," Emma said, pointing at the plate. "What do you think?"

What I thought was that she'd given me way too many cookies, but I didn't want to say so.

"They're very healthy tasting," I said.

"Jim's real pleased that you're going to be working here this summer," Emma said. "I am too. But I think we should get some things straight right off, so you'll know what you might be getting into."

"Okay," I said, but not too clearly, due to flax being hard to chew.

"I know what your dad says about me," Emma said. "Jim and I go places, and there's always somebody wondering why Jim has anything to do with me. My whole family is messed up. My dad took off and left us when I was four, and my mom had all these boyfriends that used to beat us around. My sister got pregnant when she was sixteen, and I don't even know where she is anymore. And I ran around with a lot of guys and did a lot of stupid-ass stuff I shouldn't have done. I didn't even finish high school. I dropped out my junior year."

"That sounds great to me," I said.

"Well, it wasn't," Emma said. "But I hated high

school. The kids were mean and the teachers were mean and my guidance counselor made it pretty clear that she didn't think I was heading for anything but six kids and welfare. I was probably pretty hateful too, if you want to know the truth. The only one nice to me was Miss Walker."

"She talked at Eli's funeral," I said.

Emma said, "She's something else, Miss Walker. When she heard I was quitting school, she asked me over to her house. She made Earl Grey tea. Like I would know from Earl Grey tea."

I knew Earl Grey tea due to it being the drink of Captain Jean-Luc Picard of *Star Trek*'s starship *Enterprise.* Though at home we have Lipton's.

"It was real nice," Emma said. "She didn't try to talk me into anything or out of anything, and she didn't act like a teacher. We just talked. And she gave me a copy of *The Secret Garden*. She said everybody has a special book, and she thought maybe that one might be mine."

I thought about what might be my special book.

Probably one of those pathetic old kindergarten readers with little stories about seeing Spot run.

"So what's it about?" I said.

"It's just an old kids' book," Emma said. "It's about this girl, Mary, who comes from India to live in a big old house in England. Her parents are dead and her guardian doesn't care about her and she just hates everything. Then she finds this locked garden and she finds a way to get inside and she starts bringing the garden back to life. And by the end of the book, she's saved the garden and she's saved her whiny little crippled-up cousin and she's saved herself too."

"That's your special book?" I said.

"It's what I thought of right off when Jim told me about the farm," she said.

She took a bite of flax cookie and chewed for a long time.

"I met Jim when I was waiting on tables at Bev's Caf," Emma said.

Bev's Caf used to be Bev's Café, but the *é* fell off the sign and nobody ever bothered to put it up again, so ever since it's just been Bev's Caf. Anybody who wants to get elected to something or to collect money for something always starts out at Bev's Caf, and it's where you put a sign up if you've lost a cat or a dog, and where all the kids go after prom or graduation or a football game. My mom and dad got engaged at Bev's Caf. Every year they used to go back on their engagement anniversary and play "Some Enchanted Evening" on Bev's extremely old jukebox, and split a bottle of wine. One anniversary Eli and Jim sneaked up under Bev's window and serenaded them on trombones. Eli and Jim were the entire trombone section in the Fairfield High School Orchestra and Band.

Emma said, "Jim'd come in all the time and sit in one of the booths, and I thought he was nice. Quiet, but nice. Not that we talked about anything much but the weather and did he want another cup of coffee and how about the special on pie. But I could tell. Then one day I just got up the nerve and asked what all he was doing now that he wasn't going to college anymore, and he said, why didn't we go someplace when I got off work and he'd tell me. That's when I heard all about the farm. And I thought it was just like *The Secret Garden*, you know? How there he'd been, all screwed up, and then he started growing things. And I thought I wished I could do that too. I think I fell in love with him right then."

Then she asked if I'd like another cookie, but I said no, thanks, because I'd had enough flax for one day.

"Jim told me all about what happened, how bad off he was," Emma said. "He said your brother never gave up on him. Jim thought an awful lot of your brother. He says it's because of your brother that he's still alive."

I think that's the real reason my dad doesn't like Jim.

Because Eli's dead and Jim is still alive.

CHAPTER 9

ANNE WHEELER (1833–1839)
ELIZABETH WHEELER (1831–1839)
ENOCH WHEELER (1835–1839)
MARIAH WHEELER (1836–1839)
SAMUEL WHEELER (1838–1839)
From the Cemetery Hill Graveyard

Daniel (E.) Anderson's Book of the Dead

I became friends with Walter in the graveyard.

I used to stop by Eli's grave every once in a while, and if nobody was around, I'd sit down and shoot the breeze and catch him up on stuff.

If you spend enough time in a graveyard, you really get to know the place like you do any other neighborhood. Pretty soon you even have your favorite graves. Mine were Beloved Henry, who got kicked by a horse at the age of six and ended up with a smirky little marble lamb, and Amos Pettigrew, who had a creepy carved skull and a badass epitaph:

Here lies AMOS PETTIGREW
As I am now, so shall you be
Prepare for death and follow me

Gee, thanks, Amos, I used to think, but I visited him anyway. I bet in life he didn't have many pals.

The most interesting graves were in the old cemetery, which you could get to from the new one by stepping over the fence, which wasn't hard, since most of it was lying on its side. That's where the five little Wheeler kids were, and theirs were some of my favorite graves too. I used to go over and sit on the big Wheeler-parent gravestone and look at all those little stones lined up beside it like a row of granite ducklings.

SAFE IN THE ARMS OF THE ANGELS, the big parent stone said.

I wondered what the angels had been doing while

whatever happened to the little Wheeler kids was happening, like lightning or bears or bubonic plague. Not doing their guardian-angel thing—that was pretty obvious. Maybe they'd all been goofing off at some celestial harp jam.

I was so wrapped up in blasphemous anti-angel thoughts that when this voice behind me said, "Hi, Danny," I nearly jumped out of my skin. The first thing I thought was *Zombies!* which goes to show the kind of thing you're primed for if you've spent Halloween at Peter Reilly's house with the lights out, watching *Night of the Living Dead.*

But when I turned around, it was just old weird Walter, in a pair of ratty corduroy pants and geeky high-top sneakers and that haircut that made it look like his head had been chewed by squirrels.

"I didn't mean to scare you," Walter said. "I thought you heard me."

"You didn't scare me," I said. Lying slightly.

"I see you up here a lot," Walter said. "But I figured you wanted to be alone. Most people in a graveyard want to be left alone. I can leave if you want me to. Do you want me to leave you to be alone?"

"No, that's okay," I said. "Stick around."

Walter sat down across from me on Jedediah Kimball, 1857–1904, who was now IN A BETTER PLACE. His corduroys rode up to show white socks and some white hairy leg. You could tell Walter was the type who would never get a tan.

I pointed at all the little Wheeler stones.

"What do you suppose they died of, all at once like that?"

"Diphtheria," Walter said. "Before inoculations, it sometimes killed eighty percent of children under ten."

His eyes started doing that back-and-forth thing. I know now that it was the cerebral manipulation of information, but at the time I figured he was having an epileptic fit. I'd heard about epileptic fits, and I knew that if somebody had one, you were supposed to put a stick in their mouth to keep them from biting off their tongue. But just as I started looking around for a good strong stick, Walter started talking again.

"It makes you think," Walter said. "All the scrambling around and worrying and stuff we do. And then we die. We're gone, just like that. And we think all the time that it matters, all the stuff we do, when the truth is that we're all nothing anyway. Mathematically speaking."

I realized right then that I'd been hanging around with the twins too much because the first thing I thought was that if Walter was a Pooh character, he'd be that depressing donkey. Eeyore.

"What do you mean, we're all nothing?" I said.

Walter said, "The universe has maybe a hundred billion galaxies in it. And each of those galaxies has somewhere between a billion and a trillion stars."

"Yeah?" I said.

Walter said, "And orbiting around just one of those trillions and trillions of stars is our planet, which has six billion people on it. We're like dust spots on a dust spot in the middle of a dust spot. Mathematically speaking, we average out to absolutely nothing."

Mathematically speaking is one of Walter's expressions.

I knew there was a good reason I hated math.

"You know what else?" Walter said. "There's a philosopher who thinks maybe we're not even here at all. He says our whole reality might be a computer game played by some incredibly advanced civilization. You know, like we're the Sims."

"That's nuts," I said.

But I could feel myself starting to worry about the time when I took the ladder out of the Sims' little swimming pool and just left them to swim back and forth until they croaked.

Then I thought how pissed I'd be if that turned out to be true and Eli died because some dumb-ass Little Green Kid from Alpha Centauri got bored and clicked DELETE.

Walter got down off Jedediah, walked over, and started poking with his high-top sneaker at the little Wheeler graves.

"What do you think happens after we die?" I said.

Walter got that struggle expression people get when you've asked them an awkward question and they're about to give you an answer you don't want to hear.

"Nothing," Walter said finally. "I think once the brain stops working, we cease to exist and all the molecules and atoms that we're made of drift off to become part of something else."

"Like what kind of something else?" I said. "Like reincarnation?"

Walter rolled his eyes and kept poking the grass with his toe.

"Like recycling," he said. "Like grass. Squirrels. Worms."

I thought Eli might like to be part of a squirrel. Or maybe a bird. Eli always said if he could have one X-gene mutant superpower, he'd like to be able to fly.

"What about your soul?" I said. "Don't you believe in souls?"

Pastor Jay and the Methodist Sunday School had been pretty definitive on the subject of souls.

"Look, you asked me," Walter said. "I'm not saying

there's no heaven full of people running through fields of flowers. I'm just saying what I think, is all."

"Hey. That's cool," I said.

"Not usually, it isn't," Walter said.

He grinned at me suddenly, and I saw that he had this crookedy grin that went up a little bit more on one side than the other, just like Eli's. I realized I'd never seen Walter smile before.

I guess that was when Walter and I became friends.

Things Walter loves are irrational numbers, Big Bang theory, Rube Goldberg machines, chess, licorice, Linux, the Grand Canyon, the M13 galaxy, octopuses, graphing calculators, Dr Pepper, and the Periodic Table of Elements. Things he hates are nonserious people, astrology, baseball caps on people who aren't playing baseball, Mickey Mouse, the British royal family, Twinkies, lima beans, social events, homeopathy, and preemptive war. The people he admires are Isaac Newton, James Clerk Maxwell, Alan Turing, Albert Einstein, and Bertrand Russell.

And the guy who wrote *The Hitchhiker's Guide to the Galaxy*.

I know that because in his Facebook picture he's got two heads and he claims his name is Zaphod Beeblebrox.

CHAPTER 10

VALYA STARIKOVA (1931–1944)
Eaten by wolves.
....
Daniel (E.) Anderson's Book of the Dead

Walter and Isabelle and I started hanging out together that summer because of the twins and werewolves and the full moon.

Once I started working at the Blue Potato, the twins would come out to the farm every day and eat Emma's weird cookies and hang around with the goats and the chickens and try to con Jim into letting them drive his secondhand John Deere. Jim never fell for it, even though Jasper was pretty convincing about being an expert with heavy machinery, which I think proves that Jim's brain isn't as fried as my dad says it is.

"Will those potatoes turn your tongue blue when you eat them?" Journey said, hanging over the fence where I was hoeing. "Like drinking grape Kool-Aid turns your tongue purple?"

Journey was wearing rhinestone sunglasses, overall shorts, and pink ballet slippers. Jasper was wearing cowboy boots and a T-shirt that said COME TO THE DARK SIDE. WE HAVE COOKIES.

Journey stuck out her tongue at Jasper, who stuck out his tongue back.

"No," I said. "They do not turn your tongue blue."

"I thought they'd turn your tongue blue," Journey said mournfully.

"Well, they don't," I said.

I turned around so that my back was to the twins and hoed harder, but they didn't take the hint and go away.

"We wondered if you might want to come over to our house tomorrow night," Jasper said. "Isabelle said to ask you."

My heart gave a sort of electric thunk.

"She said to ask you day before yesterday," Journey said. "But Jasper forgot to tell you. Jasper is very forgetful. If you could see the inside of Jasper's brain, it would be full of soft, fluffy balls of wool."

In microseconds I thought of several creative awful things I'd like to do to Jasper's soft woolly forgetful brain.

"If you could see the inside of *Journey*'s brain," Jasper said, "it would be full of razor blades."

Walter says that the twins are the conversational equivalent of a computer virus.

"Our parents think it's good that Isabelle is showing social interests," Jasper said. "When our dad said we were spending the summer here, she said oh, no, she wasn't. She said she wasn't going to go to some stupid little podunk town that didn't even have a symphony or an art museum. She wanted to stay in New York and live by herself in a hotel."

"Like Eloise," Journey said. "Eloise is a girl in a famous picture book. She lived in the Plaza Hotel in New York and got her meals from room service and had a pet turtle who ate raisins. But Isabelle couldn't do that because we don't have enough money for a hotel."

"Have you ever had a pet turtle?" asked Jasper.

"No," I said.

"So are you going to come over tomorrow?" Jasper said.

"It's because of the full moon," Journey said, bouncing up and down on the fence. "There's a full moon tomorrow night. Isabelle has a thing about the full moon."

"If Journey was in outer space," Jasper said, "she would not be the moon. She would be an Apollo object. That's an asteroid that's aimed at smashing into the Earth and destroying all life as we know it."

"If *Jasper* was in outer space," Journey said, "he would be puny pathetic cosmic dust."

"What *time* tomorrow?" I said. Resisting a natural impulse to hit them with the hoe.

"Seven thirty," Journey said. "I'll give Isabelle your R.S.V.P. That's how you answer an invitation. It stands for *Répondez, s'il vous plaît.* That means

'Answer, please,' in French. Did I say that I can speak French?"

"You said it," Jasper said. "You say it a lot. But you can't."

"Also Jasper might turn into a werewolf," Journey said.

"I have all the signs," Jasper said. "Like I have unusually long middle fingers." He showed me his hands and spread out his fingers. "See?"

"No," I said.

"And my ears are a little pointed, and I'm pale," Jasper said. "Werewolves are always pale."

"That's vampires," I said. "Vampires are always pale. Werewolves are toothy and hairy. Nobody wants to be around a werewolf."

I thought of Valya Starikova, this Russian kid in my Book of the Dead. She was dragged into the forest and eaten by wolves. Nothing was left but pieces of her shoes.

"Yeah," Journey said. "Because werewolves bite. Like this." And she started to gnaw on Jasper's arm.

Jasper began to yell.

Then Journey said, "I'll go tell Isabelle!" and cut off running toward the road, and Jasper hollered, "No, *I'll* tell her!" and went batting off after her.

So I went back to hoeing and hoed blue potatoes so fast that I came close to hoeing off my toes. I was that excited about having an invitation from Isabelle.

It was just lousy timing that right then Peter Reilly called up to see if I wanted to go to the movies that next night, because his brother, Tony, was going to drive him and Amanda into Fairfield and if I came along, Amanda would bring her girlfriend Yvonne Boudreau, who has a belly-button ring and blue hair. Any other time I would have wanted to go. The blue hair makes Yvonne look like a Martian, but a cute Martian, and she talks a lot, which means you don't have to say much but can just nod every once in a while and think about your own stuff and look at her chest.

Peter got ticked off when I said no, I was busy.

"Busy with *what*?" he said. "What have you got to be busy with?"

I didn't want to tell him, but he kept at it until finally I said, "I promised I'd go over to the neighbors'."

Then Peter wanted to know which neighbors and what were we going to do there, and I said it was sort of like a club meeting, which was the only thing I could think of to get him off my back. I've always been a lousy liar, which is one of the things Eli was always saying we had to work on someday. When he got back from Iraq, he said, we'd devote a whole Education Day to deception and prevarication.

Peter said I sounded stupid, and what was wrong with me and was I turning into a douche, and then he hung up. Which is because the only kind of club Peter knows about is the one his father goes to at the VFW on Friday nights to drink Jim Beam and play poker.

By Saturday, though, I was so nervous that I wished maybe I'd just *répondez-vous*-ed no to the twins and gone to the movies with Peter and Amanda and blue Yvonne. By seven, I'd changed my clothes three times, brushed my teeth twice, and had had a lot of time to get myself all worked up thinking about what a loser I was going to look like in front of Isabelle, what with not knowing what month I'd be if I was a month and not having a favorite poem.

Then I decided that if things went really wrong, I'd just run away from home and come up with a new identity, like those people in witness-protection programs. I'd go someplace really far away, like Cincinnati, and I'd pretend to have lost my memory, which always works for people in the movies. I doubted anybody would even bother to look for me, because frankly I figured my parents would be relieved.

Actually that all made me feel better, because like Eli always said, it's always important to have a backup plan. Later I told Walter about it, and he said "Great scheme, Danny," in a way that told me it wasn't.

I told my mom where I was going and she said "Fine" without looking away from where she was not exactly watching the TV, in the sort of voice that showed she really wasn't paying any attention. It left me wondering, the way I always did, if she'd say anything different if I said, "Well, good night, Mom, I'm going out to knock over a liquor store," or, "Gee, I've made this cool parachute out of an umbrella and I'm going to go jump off the Matteson River Bridge and see if it works," or, "Good-bye, Mom, I've decided to move to Timbuktu."

She didn't used to be this way. When Eli was home, we'd go out to the kitchen most nights and help Mom make dinner, and she'd say, "Well, tell me things, boys; I haven't seen you for hours." And after Eli left for college, she was the same, even though then it was just her and me.

Now I think she wouldn't even notice if I dropped dead right there on the floor. Like those people in city apartments who die and nobody realizes it for years. Or until there's a smell.

Once last year I didn't talk at all for three whole days, just to see what would happen. Nothing did. Which just goes to show.

I waited until twenty past seven, because I didn't want to be too early, because it's not cool to be early. Then I took a flashlight, because even though it was still light out, being summer, I knew I'd be coming home in the dark, and also by my third change of clothes I was wearing a black T-shirt, which doesn't show up on the road if a pickup truck comes along with somebody like Timmy Sperdle in it, full up to the eyeballs with testosterone and Coors. Then I headed off for the Sowers house.

CHAPTER 11

LI PO (701–762)
Drowned.

....

Daniel (E.) Anderson's Book of the Dead

As long as I can remember, the Sowers house has been empty, just sitting there with its wood rot and its bats and the irreversible water damage happening to the grand piano that nobody ever bothered to move out of the parlor. There's something spooky that happens with old empty houses, especially houses that are empty of people but still have all the furniture in them. I think that's what brings ghosts. When you leave things the way they were, so that nothing changes in what they left behind.

Jim Pilcher said that when he was a kid, his uncle Steve put a twenty-dollar bill in the Sowers house, on this big old carved chest of drawers in one of the bedrooms upstairs, and said anybody could have it who would go into the house and get it, all alone at midnight.

"Did anybody ever get it?" I said.

"Not on your ever-loving life," Jim said. "I gave it my best shot, thinking I could sure use a nice crisp twenty-dollar bill, and besides it would have been fun to shake it under my uncle Steve's nose. So I went out to the house and I got the front door open, which freaked me out right there, because it squeaked and creaked something fierce, and then I got into the front hall — have you even been in the Sowers house front hall?"

"Yeah," I said. "But not in the dark."

"Well, it's spooky as hell in the dark," Jim said. "All these weird shadows and big black looming stuff that you can't tell what it is. And then that hall chandelier — you remember that chandelier?"

"With all those glass prism things," I said.

"So I'm just standing there in the front hall," Jim said, "and all those little bits of prisms suddenly started shaking and shivering and clinking around, and I knew it wasn't anything I'd done. It was like somebody was walking around right over it, upstairs. I didn't like that one bit, but I took another step or two, because I still wanted to put one over on my uncle Steve. But then I heard what sounded like one of the stairs up above from the second floor creak — real loud, like somebody or something was stepping on it, coming down. And that was enough for me."

"What did you do?" I said.

"What did I do?" Jim said. "I took off running, and believe me, you've never seen anybody run so fast outside of the Summer Olympics."

Now, though, the house looked all lived in and warm, with yellow lights in the windows, and not the least full of ghosts. I figured any specter creaking around inside it would have been scared off by now by the twins. There were candles burning on the porch, the kind that are supposed to keep mosquitoes away but don't very well, at least not around here, because our mosquitoes are too tough for citronella.

"You're late," Journey said.

The twins were sitting side by side on the porch steps, looking fairly human, so nobody had turned into a werewolf yet. Journey was wearing a yellow taffeta party dress and a pair of green rubber boots with frog faces on the toes. Jasper was wearing two left sneakers and a T-shirt that said I FIGHT ZOMBIES IN MY SPARE TIME.

"You know that you guys have a very unusual fashion sense?" I said.

"We were watching for you," Jasper said. "But we didn't see you because you're wearing black like a spy."

"If you were a captured spy," Journey said, "would you rather be hanged by the neck until dead or shot by a firing squad?"

"Or sizzled up in the electric chair?" Jasper said.

"I'd rather not be captured," I said.

"Shut up, twins," Isabelle said. "Come on, Danny. Come up here and sit down."

She was sitting in a wicker rocking chair and wearing one of those Indian-print skirts and a white top with skinny straps and silver earrings the size of hockey pucks. And she had those blue, blue eyes. Isabelle always took my breath away.

"You know Walter, don't you?" Isabelle said.

And there on the other side of her was old weird Walter with his too-short pants and his chewed-up haircut, sitting on a little wicker stool so that his knees bent up practically to his ears.

It's something you can't explain exactly, why people become friends. It's chemistry, is what they say. Maybe it's just being the right people with the right feelings in the right place at the right time. But whatever it is, that summer Walter and Isabelle and I had it. And maybe even the twins too.

I wish I'd written down somewhere everything we talked about that night on Isabelle's porch. At the time I thought I'd always remember, but then I didn't, and now all that's left of those conversations is a sort of flavor of something special and exciting and strange.

What I usually talked about with Peter Reilly and Mickey Roberts and Ryan Baker and all the rest was stuff like the Yankees and the Red Sox and the kind of motorcycle Peter was going to buy someday, when he had enough money to buy a motorcycle, and what really happened at the end of the *Sopranos* and who was dating who from school.

But with Walter and Isabelle and me, it was different. We talked about things that meant something. And we all listened to each other too, which, if you think about it, is rare. In most conversations, people don't really listen. They just wait for you to be done talking and shut up so that they can say something of their own. Or they shut you up before you even begin, like my dad does.

All the time we were talking, the twins were running around in the grass chasing fireflies, which were blinking on and off all over the place like crazy things. Fireflies were new to them, due to there not being any in apartments in New York City.

"They're magic," Isabelle said. "They're like little bits of stars."

Then Walter, who sometimes can't help himself, said that firefly light was really the result of an enzymatic reaction and that fireflies weren't flies anyway, but beetles. I was worried that Isabelle would get upset with that, because even though Walter is a genius, his explanations can be real downers sometimes, but instead she just started to laugh.

"I'm not listening, darling," Isabelle said, and she put her fingers in her ears.

It was right then on Isabelle's porch, with the citronella candles with their fake-lemon smell and the creaking sound of rocking chairs, that I knew something was happening. That my life was beginning to change.

I knew that if at the lunch table at school, I told Peter and Mickey and Ryan and everybody that Walter was a really cool guy and we should have him come over and sit with us, they'd hoot and boo and laugh until milk came out of their noses and ask what I'd been smoking or if I'd been popping pills. They wouldn't care that Walter knew all about parallel universes and philosophy and art and literature and beetles and all, because they wouldn't see anything but that stupid haircut and that thing he does with his eyes.

I also knew if I took my tray over to sit with Walter, I might as well kiss my social life good-bye. Like my dad said, people judge you by your friends.

But something was changing all the same.

"Do you know how you can tell what a person's truly like?" Isabelle said.

I said no and Walter said the Myers-Briggs Personality Test.

"No, darlings, it's by their auras," Isabelle said. "I learned to read them last year from this very spiritual woman, a holistic theologist, who teaches courses online. Your aura is the manifestation of your true nature. It's why you see halos on angels and saints. Halos are really just very intense auras. On ordinary people, they're smaller and paler."

I could tell from Walter's conflicted expression that he didn't believe a word of this but didn't want to contradict Isabelle.

"Come in the house for a minute and I'll read yours," Isabelle said. "You have to stand up against a plain white wall."

The old Sowers house was really grand. The front hall had a marble floor laid out in squares, like a black-and-white checkerboard, and a huge curving staircase like something out of *Gone With the Wind* that went up to a landing with a big gold-framed mirror and then split into two staircases, one going right and the other left. Some of the spindles were broken out of the banister, and the red carpet was shabby, but you could still imagine what it must have been like at the old Sowers parties, with men in fancy suits with striped pants and women all glittering in diamonds and satin gowns.

Off to one side there was a little parlor, where Isabelle's parents were sitting on a couch with the stuffing coming out, drinking something out of teacups and watching a news program on this very small television set. She introduced us and we all said hi. Isabelle's father was more athletic looking than I would have expected from a professor, and Isabelle's mother looked a little bit like Isabelle, but tireder, which was probably due to living with the twins.

Then Isabelle showed us the room where her father was writing his monograph, which had a big mahogany desk with a computer on it and piles of books and papers, and the room where her mother did her interpretive paintings. The paintings were propped up around the walls and were all in shades of purple and orange and looked like no cows that I'd ever seen.

"It's a series. She's calling it *Atomic Moo*," Isabelle said. "She's going to have a show next winter in New York."

Which, though I did not say so to Isabelle, is the only place you could show cube-shaped orange cows without everybody laughing themselves sick. People in New York don't know beans about cows.

Then she took us out to the kitchen, which had an old iron coal stove the size of a steam locomotive, with a new microwave perched on top of it, and then through to the butler's pantry, which was mostly empty except for a couple of soup tureens big enough for baby baths.

"This is the only room in the house that has a

plain white wall," Isabelle said. "Stand over there. This will take a minute."

So Walter and I stood against the plain white wall, and Isabelle took a few steps back, took a deep breath, and squinted at us.

She looked so beautiful standing there, and I thought that if Isabelle had an aura, it would probably be all silver and glowing like moonbeams and new snow.

She stared and stared until I started to fidget. Then she said, "There!"

"What?" I said.

"Yours is royal blue, Walter," Isabelle said. "That means you have a strong balanced existence and you're transmitting a lot of good energy."

Walter said "Umf" in a noncommittal sort of way that managed to sound pleased and skeptical at the same time.

My aura wasn't blue. It was yellowish brown.

"What does that mean?" I said.

"It means that your life is in difficulty," Isabelle said. "Your psyche is suffused with pain and anger."

127

Great, I thought. I felt like I'd flunked another math test. I could feel that aura hanging around me, full of bad energy and looking like old mustard.

Then the twins came busting in, yelling that we had to come out and see the moon, and so we all went back outside again.

And it was one fantastic full moon.

It was so bright that it made shadows on the grass. Everything looked all glazed with moonlight like sugar frosting, the trees and the bushes and the grass and the porch steps and the stone pillars at the end of the drive. And it was huge, like something out of a science-fiction movie. Like the moon the kid rode past on his bicycle in *E.T.* when the alien made everybody fly. It was so fantastic that I almost forgot I had an aura the color of baby poop.

"I think I'm turning into a werewolf," Jasper said. "I feel itchy all over. I think I'm growing fur."

"I think you're not," Isabelle said.

"And my eyes feel hot," Jasper said. "My eyes feel really hot. Do my eyes look glowing and yellow? Like the eyes of a fierce wild animal?"

"No," I said.

"I feel an urge to howl," Jasper said.

"I feel an urge to howl too," Journey said.

"I feel a need for silver bullets," Isabelle said.

The twins started running around and howling, "AaaOOOOOO! AaaOOOOOO!" They sounded like wolf cubs who had maybe had their tails slammed in a door.

Isabelle said, "When I was little, I thought there were Moon Elves. I thought they'd fly down to earth on nights when the moon was full and perch on my windowsill. They had silver wings and silver hair and pearl-colored eyes, and they made little cheeping sounds like baby birds. I used to leave them things I thought they'd like to eat. Moon food. Necco wafers and dragées — you know, those little silver balls they use to decorate wedding cakes."

We all looked at the moon.

I said, "When I was little, my mom showed me how to find the face of a man in the moon, but then Eli showed me how to find a rabbit, and after that all I could see was that rabbit."

Walter said that there wasn't any man or rabbit.

Walter has a very limited moon. All he sees are the Mare Imbrium, the Mare Tranquillitatis, the Oceanus Procellarum, and the Tycho ray crater.

Isabelle said, "Later I used to worry about the Moon Elves, that they'd gone away because I'd grown up. Like Wendy did in *Peter Pan*. I always thought that part was so sad, when Peter comes back for her, years later, and she's too old to go back with him to Neverland."

For a moment she looked sad, and then an instant later she was laughing again, and she threw up her arms and shouted, "Moon Elves! It's me, Isabelle! Come back! Come back! I'm still here!"

And suddenly I remembered Eli. You know how memory sometimes comes in flashes, like a little video clip in your brain? Just a little piece of something, and you can't remember what happened before or after, but the middle bit is really clear? I remembered sitting on the back porch steps with Eli and looking at the stars.

Clear nights where we are, it looks like there's

a million stars, though Walter, who has probably counted them and done a statistical analysis, says only six thousand are visible to the naked eye. But it sure seems like a lot more. There are so many, and they're so far away, that it's hard to look up at them without realizing that you're really pretty incredibly small. Like Walter says, mathematically we're nothing.

So Eli and I are sitting there, and there are peepers peeping — *squee-squee-squee* — like tiny little accordions, and fireflies blinking greeny yellow, and the Big Dipper dangling down over the barn, and I'm feeling small. Maybe Eli was too, because all of a sudden he jumped up and started to yell.

"Hey, universe! It's me, Eli! I'm here!"

And he grabbed me and yanked me up.

"Come on, Danny! Make first contact!" he said.

So then we're both yelling up at the sky, "I'm here! I'm here!"

Like the tiny little people in that Dr. Seuss book, *Horton Hears a Who!*

Suddenly I missed Eli so much that my stomach

twisted up. I thought how I'd do anything to have him back again, even just for five minutes. Even for two.

"Danny?" Walter said. "Are you okay?"

"Yeah," I said. "Sure."

"Let's dance!" Isabelle said.

She ran out into the grass and started spinning around and around on her bare feet in the moonlight, with her arms held out and her silky hair flying and her Indian skirt flaring around her knees, so that she looked like a twirling silvery flower.

So the twins stopped howling and started spinning too, and then so did I, and even geeky Walter, looking like a gawky human windmill, and then we were all spinning around and around together under that huge silver moon. To look at us, you'd think the moonlight had made us all crazy.

Walter says that in ancient times, people believed that moonlight did make you insane, which is why words like *lunacy* and *lunatic* come from *luna*, which is Latin for "moon." You even got a lighter sentence for a crime if you committed it while there was a full moon. Which frankly gave me some ideas involving Mr. Engelmann, who teaches Algebra I.

In this case, though, it wasn't just the moonlight. It was Isabelle.

Finally we got so dizzy with all the spinning that we just fell over in the grass, everybody laughing like zanies, and lay there, getting sopped by the dew and staring up at the spinning stars. I could hear the twins, who had fallen over on top of each other next to me, bickering about what stars would taste like if you could eat them, and Journey thought they'd be fizzy like ginger ale and Jasper thought they'd be tangy like lime sherbet, and then Journey said she thought she was going to throw up, but luckily she didn't.

Isabelle reached out and touched my hand.

"Let's always be like this," Isabelle said. "Let's be wild and free and young. Let's believe in magic and wishing wells and fairy godmothers and love at first sight and doors in closets that take you into Narnia."

"If Journey was in Narnia, she would be the White Witch," Jasper said.

Isabelle wrapped her fingers around my hand and squeezed.

"Let's promise that we'll come back here to this very spot fifty years from now and we'll dance in the moonlight again, all of us, because even when we're old, we won't have changed. Promise that we'll never change."

"Never," I said. I would have promised her anything.

"Let's always remember this night," Isabelle said. "Let's memorize everything about it so that we'll never ever forget it and all the rest of our lives we'll be able to close our eyes and it will come back to us just the way it was."

So we lay there memorizing, which must have worked, because I can still remember how that night smelled of wet grass and roses and maybe a little whiff of pig manure, with the twins giggling and poking at each other, and Isabelle lying there, gleaming, with one arm behind her head, and Walter with his big bony knees bent up and his glasses white with moonlight.

The full moon always makes me think of Isabelle.

But at the same time I think about Li Po from my Book of the Dead. Li Po was an ancient Chinese poet who wrote more than a thousand poems, many of which involved heavy drinking. He was known as one of the Eight Immortals of the Wine Cup. One night, after a whole lot of wine cups, he drowned when he jumped into the Yangtze River, trying to embrace the reflection of the moon.

Thinking back, I guess that was what I was like with Isabelle, except without the cups of wine.

The truth is that everything always changes.

And some things you just can't have.

CHAPTER 12

PRINCE ALBERT OF SAXE-COBURG-GOTHA
(1819–1861)
Died of typhoid fever.
....
Daniel (E.) Anderson's Book of the Dead

Walter's least favorite period of history is the Dark Ages, due to bubonic plague, lack of computers, general ignorance, and the divine right of kings.

Isabelle's least favorite is the Victorian era, due to whalebone corsets, turgid novels, and the unavailability of birth control.

This last was why Queen Victoria and Prince Albert had nine kids. Queen Victoria lived to be eighty-one, but Prince Albert died of typhoid at the age of forty-two. The queen never got over his death. She wore nothing but black for the rest of her life. She even pretended that Albert was still around.

She ordered the maids to lay out fresh clothes for him every morning and to bring hot shaving water to his room. Visitors to the palace still had to sign Albert's guest book as well as the queen's, so he could see who had come to call. Everything was kept as if he was still alive and had maybe just gone out for a stroll around the garden before lunch. It was like the death version of "The Emperor's New Clothes." I mean, everybody knew Albert was dead as a doornail, but they pretended right along with the queen.

That's what my mom did too, with Eli. Everything in his room was just the way he left it. All his clothes were still in his bureau drawers or on hangers in his closet, and his posters were still on the wall, along with the big tacked-up piece of brown paper that he used for writing down messages and phone numbers and important thoughts. His brown paper said things like "Jar Jar Binks Must Die!"

His clock radio was still set for his favorite station, though it never came on anymore, and all his books were still in his bookcase. Even the couple of books he'd had on his bedside table when he went off to war were still right where he'd left them, with the bookmarks stuck in them.

I didn't go in there anymore, though, because once when I did, rummaging around for a pencil, my mom totally freaked. She came running down the hall with her bathrobe undone and her hair snarled up and witchy and her eyes all wild.

"What are you doing in here?" she said. Then she said it again, louder. *"What are you doing in here?"*

And then when she saw the open desk drawer, she yelled, *"Don't touch his things!"*

"It's just a pencil," I said. "Eli wouldn't care."

"Leave it *alone!*" she said. "Get away from there, Danny! Don't come in here!"

And her face got all red and splotchy, and she shoved me out of the room and slammed the door.

I used to wish that Eli would come back as a ghost. I figured I'd be the only one who could see him, because kids are sensitive to ghosts, like that kid in the movie *Sixth Sense* who could see dead people. I imagined him sitting at the end of my bed, maybe looking a little transparent and soap bubbly, the way ghosts do, and thought how we'd still be able to talk to each other, even though nobody would be able to hear him but me. Like Ghost Eli would be my secret invisible friend.

Then I realized how it would suck to be a ghost. I mean, what do ghosts do all day? It's not like they can have friends or a career. Or do anything. Eli would hate it, being ectoplasm.

Which is why I hated Winnie Carver, the Psychic Medium.

Winnie Carver had a late-night call-in radio show called *The Other Side*. It began with this spooky *Twilight Zone* music, and then a whispery voice said: *"The spirits of the dead are all around us. They wait beyond the veil, watching, yearning to speak to the loved ones they have left behind. Join us tonight with psychic medium Winnie Carver and listen to the voices calling out to you, calling from . . . the Other Side."* Then a brisk nonspooky nonwhispery voice gave the radio-show call-in phone number and explained how Winnie Carver was also available for personal appointments.

In her normal mind, my mom would never have fallen for somebody like Winnie Carver, but after Eli died, my mom was pretty much cracked. Walter says this isn't surprising. For example, after the Civil War, due to the bereaved being mentally unbalanced by loss and grief, lots of people turned to spiritualism, trying to get in touch with their dead husbands and sons.

My mom would go off and see Winnie Carver and then she'd come home and shut herself up in Eli's room and then she and my dad would fight.

"This is insane, Ellen!" my dad would shout through the door. "That woman is a fraud! Do you know what she *charges*? She charges a goddamn fortune! And she's not talking to your son, Ellen! It's a scam! You hear me? It's a big fat fake!"

Winnie Carver was one of the few things my dad and I ever agreed about, because I know what Eli would have said about Winnie Carver. Eli would have said that Winnie Carver was a steaming load of crap.

Then Isabelle came up with the Ouija board.

The whole thing was really my fault, because I gave her the idea by telling her the story about Jim Pilcher and his uncle Steve's twenty-dollar bill and the *something* that started creaking down the Sowers house stairs.

We were sitting under one of the Sowers's big old trees again, watching the twins, who were building a medieval pavilion out of a bedsheet, a bunch of tomato cages, and a pair of aluminum lawn chairs. At least they said it was a medieval pavilion.

"I *knew* the house was haunted," Isabelle said. "I knew it. I could feel a presence."

Walter opened his mouth to say something negative and scientific, but Isabelle had closed her eyes and leaned back against the tree trunk and didn't notice. Her silky hair was pulled back in a ponytail, and her eyelashes were so long that they made little shadows on her cheeks.

"But I sense that it's a friendly ghost," Isabelle said. "A lonely little spirit that means us no harm."

She sat up abruptly.

"Let's try to contact it," she said. Her face lit up

and her blue eyes sparkled. "Think how incredible it would be if we could actually talk to it."

"And just how would we do that?" Walter said.

"With the Ouija board," Isabelle said. "It's a gateway to the spirit realm. Did you know that this woman Emily Hutchings wrote a novel that was dictated to her through the Ouija board by Mark Twain? I read about it on Wikipedia."

Walter opened his mouth again, but Isabelle reached out to either side and put a hand on each of our knees.

"Please?" she said. "Let's just try."

So we said yes because neither of us could ever resist Isabelle.

For reasons of privacy and ghost appeal, we decided to set the Ouija board up in the cupola, which is at the very top of the Sowers house, sticking up out of the roof like a decoration on top of a wedding cake, only trimmed with curlicues of white wood instead of frosting. You reach it by climbing three flights of stairs.

First there's the big fancy staircase in the front

hall, the one with the red carpet and the carved banisters, and then a steeper cheaper staircase covered with little tacked-down pieces of linoleum, and then a staircase that's practically a ladder that goes up through a hole in the cupola floor. Once you crawl through the hole, you're in this little octagon-shaped room with windows all around and some rickety old chairs, a dead plant in a pot, and a table. Isabelle had set up the Ouija board on the table. The whole place smelled of dust and dead flies.

"There's a girl at my school who lives in a haunted apartment," Isabelle said. "It's haunted by the ghost of a little girl. They hear her crying, and at night they hear her crawling around on the floor. And sometimes they can see her in mirrors. She has long yellow ringlets, and she's wearing a blue silk dress with a lace collar."

"How did she die?" I said.

"The nursemaid drowned her in the bath," Isabelle said. "She had a history of drowning children. They called her the Drowning Angel, because she said she was only sending the little ones to be angels in heaven. She was tried but never executed, for reasons of insanity."

"If she was drowned, you'd think her ghost would be wet," Walter said. "In those stories about ghosts of drowned sailors, people are always finding puddles and seaweed on the floor."

"I thought you couldn't see ghosts in mirrors," I said.

Isabelle ignored us.

She had lit candles in jars, and since by then it was dark outside, we were all reflected in the cupola windows. We looked shadowy and transparent in the glass, as if our own ghosts were floating outside in the air and staring in at us.

The twins were sitting on the floor against one wall, and Isabelle had told them that they had to be absolutely silent on pain of instant death. They both had their lips pinched tight together, which made them look like prunes. Jasper was wearing a T-shirt with a tentacle-y monster on it that said CTHULHU FOR PRESIDENT — WHY CHOOSE THE LESSER EVIL? Journey was wearing a bathing-suit top and polka-dot pajama pants. She had a pad of yellow paper on her knees and was holding a pencil.

"So what do we do?" I said.

"We all put our fingers on the planchette," Isabelle said.

It was a little heart-shaped piece of wood on wheels.

"You just rest them there — very, very lightly. And then you don't do anything. I'll ask questions, and if a spirit wants to communicate, it'll spell a message using the letters on the board. And Journey — without talking, *or else* — will write it down."

We put our fingers very, very lightly on the planchette, and I realized at once the problem with the Ouija board. I knew I could never concentrate on the spirit realm with Isabelle's fingers touching mine like that. I felt hot all over, and I started sweating on my upper lip. What if the planchette could tell how I felt? What if it suddenly started spelling out stuff like DANNY LOVES ISABELLE? Or something way more embarrassing, with sex.

"O spirits!" Isabelle said in a dramatic throaty

voice. "O spirits, please speak to us! Is there anyone there? Are there any messages for anyone here from the other side?"

We sat there with nothing happening. Isabelle had her eyes closed. Walter was glaring at the planchette, and I could tell he was still thinking about the drowned little-girl ghost who should have been dripping. Walter has trouble with logical discrepancies like that. The twins were whispering to each other, but apparently not loud enough for the pain-of-instant-death thing to click in.

"Is anyone there?" Isabelle said again.

There was a little *whoosh* of breeze through the windows, which were open at the top because it was really hot up in the cupola. The breeze made the candle flames flicker and flap like crazy things but didn't do much to cool anything down.

"Don't be afraid, O spirits!" Isabelle said. "Please come to us! Is anybody there?"

And then the planchette gave a little wiggle under our fingers and started to roll.

It rolled back and forth and back and forth, and

I knew I wasn't pushing on it, and I was pretty sure Walter wasn't, and Isabelle still had her eyes closed. Back and forth like one of those little bumper cars at the Fairfield County Fair. Then it stopped. It was pointing at the *H*. Isabelle opened up her eyes.

"*H*," she said. "Write it down, Journey. Does anyone know anybody from beyond whose name starts with *H*?"

"'*G* is for George smothered under a rug,'" Journey muttered. "'*H* is for Hector done in by a thug.'"

The twins have this morbid alphabet book about kids who came to awful ends. They both know it by heart.

"There've been a lot of Sowerses named Henry," I said.

At which point the planchette moved on to *E*.

"*E*," Isabelle said.

"'*E* is for Ernest who choked on a peach,'" Jasper stage-whispered.

Isabelle glared at him.

"What did I tell you?" she said menacingly.

147

Jasper stopped whispering and pinched up his lips.

Then the planchette whizzed across the board to *Y.*

"H-E-Y," Isabelle said. *"Hey?"*

I thought, *What kind of a ghost says "hey"?* It didn't seem like a ghost-type word.

The planchette just sat for a few seconds as if it was thinking, then swooped through three letters real fast. *K. I. D.*

HEY, KID.

And I got a crawly feeling up my back, and the hair on the back of my neck stood up on end. I yanked my fingers off that planchette so fast that you would've thought it had suddenly turned red-hot. I shoved my chair way back to get away from that board.

"That's what Eli always said," I said in a voice that didn't sound at all like me. It sounded more like Beaker, the squeaky Muppet.

Isabelle got an excited interested look, and her eyes went wide.

"Oh, God, it's your *brother*," she said. "Danny, he's *here*. He's really here. Let's see what he says. Let's ask him what it's like, where he is."

"No!" I said, still in that voice that didn't sound at all like me.

"But don't you want to *know*?" Isabelle said, incredulous. She looked really beautiful by candle-light. "He could have a *message* for you, Danny. Don't you want to hear what he has to say?"

"No," I said. "It's not him."

I didn't want it to be him.

"But *why*?" Isabelle said. "This could be a *break-through*. Danny, please. Please let's talk to him. Let's try again."

"*I'll* talk to him," Journey said.

And I realized right then why I'd really hated Winnie Carver and why I hated the Ouija board.

There was part of me deep down that kept hoping that Eli was still alive. I had a buried secret hope that it was all a mistake, the kind the army makes some-times, and that Eli wasn't dead after all but miss-ing. He'd hit his head on a rock after the bomb and lost his memory, and he'd been wandering around in the desert, maybe living with Bedouins and riding camels like Lawrence of Arabia. Eventually he'd remember who he was and he'd remember us, and then we'd get a phone call from some doctor at an army base.

"May I ask who is calling?" my mom would say, and her face would go all confused, because she wouldn't be able to take it in at first, and then when she did, she'd light up all over like a sunrise, and she'd turn to me with this incredible smile and she'd say, "It's a miracle, Danny. They've found Eli. Eli's alive. He's coming home."

Then Walter cleared his throat.

"You know how a Ouija board really works?" he said. All calm and deadpan, like Walter does. Like Mr. Spock, the voice of reason on *Star Trek*.

"No," I said. Squeaked.

"It's called the ideomotor effect," Walter said. "People make these little muscle movements all the time that they don't even realize are happening. That's what moves the planchette around the board.

You're doing it yourself even though you think you aren't. You were thinking about your brother, so unconsciously you spelled out words you used to hear him say."

Isabelle looked crushed.

"Dowsing is the same," Walter said, dry as toast. "And those mystic pendulums. You know, you dangle the pendulum over a piece of paper that has YES and NO written on it and you ask it questions and it's supposed to move toward the right answer. But it's really you who's moving it all along."

I thought how Eli used to have us ask questions all the time of the Magic 8 Ball that he got for his birthday once from Uncle Al. "Do we need a milkshake?" he'd ask that ball. Then he'd shake it up, and if it said YES, he'd say that the old Magic 8 Ball always knew, and if it said NO, he'd say that the Anderson brothers were too smart to pay any attention to a stupid plastic ball.

"But there *are* spirits," Isabelle said. "Maybe they just won't come near nonbelievers."

She eyed Walter.

"'There are more things in heaven and earth, Horatio, than are dreamt of in your philosophy.'"

"What?" I said.

"Shakespeare," Walter said.

"But what if we've actually made contact?" Isabelle said. "Do you want to turn him away? Danny?"

"It's not him," I said.

All of me was sweating now, and I knew that if I let them, my teeth would start to chatter.

Isabelle sighed, folded up the Ouija board, and started blowing out the candles. I could tell by the way she didn't look at Walter that she thought it was all Walter's fault.

"Maybe we can try again another night," she said.

But I knew I wouldn't, even for Isabelle.

We all went downstairs, and Isabelle let the twins start talking again, which ordinarily I would have thought was a huge mistake but just then was sort of a relief.

When my mom stopped seeing Winnie Carver, I'd thought it was because of my dad and the money thing. But right then I wasn't so sure. I thought that maybe a part of my mom, the real part, the part I knew, didn't want Eli out there being a ghost. She didn't want him stuck with the psychic medium any more than I wanted him trapped in some stupid Ouija board.

Because I'd rather it was what Walter said.

I'd rather it was just me.

CHAPTER 13

MAJOR GENERAL JOHN SEDGWICK (1813–1864)
Shot at the Battle of Spotsylvania Courthouse.
....
Daniel (E.) Anderson's Book of the Dead

One of the things I like best about Jim Pilcher is that he doesn't give a damn about my college plans.

There's something about being my age — it's like every adult around you has only one topic of conversation, and that's your future. What you're actually doing right now isn't important. The only thing that's important is what you're going to be doing ten years from now. What they want to know is: Where are you going to go to college? What are you going to do with your life? How are you going to make a living?

And they hate it when you say: I don't know. I don't know. I don't know.

My future was pretty much all my dad talked about when he talked to me, and I could tell he thought my prospects were bleak. Every time we discussed it, I came away knowing he figured I'd be spending my life in the Fairfield Alarm Clock factory on the third shift, sticking on the minute hands. Or maybe lying under a plastic bag in the gutter, drinking cough syrup through a straw. "Exactly what do you plan to do with your life?" my dad would say. "How are you going to support yourself? This isn't something you think about later, Daniel. This is something you think about now. If you don't apply yourself and get your grades up over the next couple of years, you're not going to have many options left. People who don't know where they're going, Daniel, are generally going nowhere. And you're not a little kid anymore. It's about time you stopped acting like one."

"Yeah," I would say.

"Yeah *what*?" my dad would say. "When Eli was your age, he'd already made a college list. He had ambitions. It's the ambitious people that go places,

Daniel, not the people who just sit on their butts, waiting for something to happen."

"Yeah, look where Eli went," I said.

"That's enough of that lip, young man," my dad said.

Walter says what I have with my dad is not a discussion. Walter says that a discussion is an informal debate between two or more people, which ours is not, due to my dad doing all the talking.

I didn't know what I wanted to do with the rest of my life, but what I did figure out that summer was that I really loved working at the blue-potato farm. Which surprised me, since I didn't take the job because I was so into farms or blue potatoes. I just wanted out of remedial summer school. But it turned out to be what Walter calls serendipity, which is stumbling across something great when you're not really looking for it.

The thing is, when you think about it, growing stuff is so cool. You start out in the spring with this puny seed the size of your pinky fingernail, and you put it in the ground and pour some water on it, and then all of a sudden you've got a million miles of vines and a bunch of pumpkins the size of beach balls. It's like one of those magician acts where they make a train appear out of nothing.

It's sort of fascinating when you think about it, why people like one thing and not another. I mean, why? Why do people like dogs more than cats or chocolate more than vanilla or art history more than chemistry?

And once you know what you like doing, why can't you just go do it? How come if all you like is computers, you have to prove you're good in American history and French before they'll let you into college to do computer science? What they say is that you have to be well rounded, which doesn't make much sense to me, seeing as there's a planet of six billion of us. It seems to me if we all just did what we're good at, the planet would average out to okay.

Anyway, Jim says I'm a natural with potatoes and also holistically connected to the earth, or at least I would be if I'd remember to keep my great big clown-foot sneakers out of his rhubarb, and Emma says I've got green thumbs.

But what Peter Reilly said that summer was that I'd lost my freaking mind.

I was still friends with Peter and the other guys, but I just didn't seem to have much time for them anymore, what with the potatoes and Jim and Emma and hanging out with Isabelle and Walter. But the more I said I was busy, the more Peter got on my case. "Busy with *what*?" he said. "What do you have to be so freaking busy with?"

Then he told me how last Saturday, he'd gone over to Amanda's house and they'd watched *Jaws 2* on DVD, the one where the shark eats a bunch of teenagers, and then they'd made out on the couch in the Turners' rec room, and Peter found out that Amanda wears black lace bras.

Then he said, what about this weekend, doing something with him and Amanda and blue Yvonne? When I said I couldn't, he got mad.

"What's the *matter* with you, Anderson?" Peter said.

Then he told me to take my head out of my ass.

Then he hung up the phone.

For a long time Peter had been my best friend and the person I most wanted to be if I could be anybody except me. But I was changing, and there wasn't anything I could do about it, any more than you can stuff a butterfly back into a cocoon and say, "Hey, big mistake; go be a caterpillar again."

One of Walter's questions is: "Can a person step into the same river twice?"

The first time he asked it, we were sitting on the bank of Scrubgrass Creek, Walter and Isabelle and me, with our feet in the water. The twins were splashing around downstream, building a beaver dam, though not nearly as effectively as beavers.

I wasn't paying as much attention to Walter as I should have been, due to thinking about how Isabelle had really beautiful feet. Neat and narrow, with these perfect little toes.

"Well, sure," I said.

And I stepped into the creek twice. *Splash. Splash.*

"Nothing to it," I said.

"No, think about it," Walter said.

So instantly I knew that I should have known better. When Walter asks a question, *Lost in Space* music should start playing in your head. You know, that movie with the robot that goes "Danger, Will Robinson, danger!"

Walter said, "The creek just keeps flowing along, so by the time you got your foot back in it, it was a whole different creek. The water you stepped in the first time is now somewhere down by the bridge. And everything about you is just a little bit changed too. You've got different air molecules in your lungs, and your blood is circulating, so now it's all in different places, and you've gotten a little bit older."

If that robot had had to deal with Walter, its head would have spun around and it would have had a software meltdown.

"Not older enough to count," I said defensively. "Only like about two seconds."

"All right," Walter said. "Are you the same person now that you were five years ago?"

I thought about how different things were five years ago. How my mom was still teaching school and cooking and telling silly jokes, and I still had a big brother and my world had felt safe and steady.

"No," I said. "I guess not."

"Five years ago," Isabelle said, "I wanted to be a wizard like in the Harry Potter books, and I was really upset that I was a Muggle. I collected heart-shaped stones and I wouldn't eat anything orange and I had this favorite hat that I wore all the time. One of those knitted Peruvian hats. You know, with earflaps and the long braided things hanging down on either side."

I thought how cute Isabelle would look in a hat with earflaps and long braided things hanging down on either side.

"I was definitely a whole different person then."

She kicked her feet in the water, and the sun caught the spray where it splashed up and turned into lots of little silver beads.

"And that was the year the twins were four and they kept insisting they were robots and they ran around making *meep-meep* noises. They wanted a cookie. *Meep-meep.* They wanted juice. *Meep-meep.* And they couldn't take baths because that would destroy their electronic insides. The only way my parents could get them to go to bed was by pretending to take their batteries out."

"I think the twins are still exactly the same people," I said.

Isabelle said, "The bar-code reader at the supermarket checkout in Fairfield goes *meep-meep*. The first time I heard it, I screeched. The sales clerk thought I was insane."

Then the twins came splashing up, yelling and pointing because most of their beaver dam was not being in the same place twice, due to having suddenly washed down the creek and gone under the bridge.

What Walter thinks is that people are like rivers. We never stay in the same place but just keep flowing along, learning new stuff and picking up new experiences and changing all the time. So today's you isn't the same as yesterday's you and won't be the same as tomorrow's you.

But Walter also thinks that there's a real perfect you that you're always trying to get to, and the better you are at living your life, the closer you come to it.

Walter is looking to the future in which he will have evolved into the Perfect Geek.

But I have to say that since Eli died, I don't have faith in the future the way I used to. I mean, how do you know you'll have one? Which is one thing I like about Jim Pilcher. He knows how that feels.

Jim says that men make plans and the mice in the ceiling laugh. That's an old Japanese saying that means that people can plan all they want, but unexpected things have a way of smashing those plans to smithereens. Then the mice giggle themselves sick. When Jim says it, he's thinking about how he went off to college with his life plan all thought out, and how Melissa Murray from Chagrin Falls, Ohio, and substance abuse shot it all to hell.

Emma says that what she thinks about plans is all in this story she got from her auntie Dell.

We were sitting on the back steps off Emma's kitchen. Emma was wearing baggy denim shorts and one of Jim's old T-shirts, and she had more freckles than ever from being out in the sun.

"Auntie Dell wasn't really our aunt," Emma said. "We all just called her that. She used to live down the street, and we'd go visit and sometimes we'd stay there overnight when my mom had a new boyfriend and didn't want us around. Anyway, one day she was all hung down and sick looking, and we said, what's wrong? And she said her daughter's boy, who was seventeen, had just got hit by a truck and killed. A real bright boy, she said, and a hard worker. He might of gone somewhere, she said.

"Then she sat us down on her saggy couch and pointed a finger right at our noses and said, 'So you girls listen good. If ever you think what you're doing isn't living, you get out of there fast. Because sooner or later there's a truck comes down the road for every one of us.'"

Emma picked up the glass I'd had my black-carrot smoothie in, the remains of which looked like something that might have oozed out of the ground at Chernobyl.

"I don't think she meant for me to drop out of school though."

But that's what I mean about the future. You can't count on it. Because you never know how much of one you're going to have.

In my Book of the Dead, there's a Major General John Sedgwick, who fought on the side of the Union in the Civil War. At the Battle of Spotsylvania in Virginia, the Confederates were shooting at his troops and his men were all jumping back and ducking behind stuff and running for cover. General Sedgwick yelled that he was ashamed of them. He said they were in no danger. He said, "Why, they couldn't hit an elephant at this dist—" Those were his last words. Right then he dropped dead with a bullet through the eye.

CHAPTER 14

THE *TITANIC* (April 15, 1912)
*People who went down in the ship: 1,495, including
14 honeymoon couples and the entire band.*
....
Daniel (E.) Anderson's Book of the Dead

Let's say you die and you go to heaven, and it turns out that you get to pick the best day in your life to live over again. What day would you pick? A birthday, a Christmas, a graduation day?

Walter wouldn't tell me his pick, because he said all the relevant data were not available yet, which means that he is not as devoted to a life of the mind as he says he is, but still has hopes of someday meeting an attractive female person who is as smart and weird as he is. Jim said it was the day he harvested his first blue-potato crop. Emma said it was the day she found out she and Jim were going to have a baby.

But I'll tell you what mine would be. Mine would be the pretty much perfect day I had with Isabelle.

Not that that's fair to Isabelle, because it started with her having her heart broken by an e-mail from Simon Dewitt Paxton, the boyfriend who was spending the summer in France. By then it was the end of July, and I knew more than I really wanted to know about Simon Dewitt Paxton. From Isabelle I knew that he was six feet two inches tall and had elegant hands and that he played the oboe and was on the school fencing team. He came from a wealthy family on Long Island and was very distantly related to Theodore Roosevelt and Cornelius Vanderbilt, and he had an uncle who was a senator.

From the twins I knew that Isabelle had a picture of him on her bedside table, along with one of those little bud vases with a rose.

"She kisses it good night," Jasper said. "Like this."

He made a kissing face. Journey pretended to throw up on his feet.

"So what's he like?" I said.

"He's very polite," Journey said. "He goes to one

of those schools where you have to wear a jacket and a tie."

"Isabelle's friend Marnie thinks he might be gay," Jasper said. "That means he might be homosexual. Do you know what homosexual is?"

"Yes," I said. I hoped Marnie was right.

"But Isabelle says that's crap," Jasper said.

"Once he locked us out in the hall," Journey said. "When he was visiting. We were out there for a whole afternoon. We played eleven games of Candy Land."

"And Journey cheated," Jasper said. "She cheated at the Lollipop Woods."

"If Jasper was a lollipop," Journey said, "he would taste like soap."

Simon had been in France for one and a half months, and he had been to the Louvre and the Arc de Triomphe and the Eiffel Tower and Notre Dame. He had also gone boating on the Seine and ordered croissants in cafés, and fallen in love with Andrée, who was the daughter of the family he was living with and who had not only helped him greatly improve his speaking knowledge of French but was very cute in a Continental sort of way that involved little black dresses and high-heeled shoes. Though of course he wanted Isabelle always to be his friend.

I knew the friend thing was a bad sign, from the Education Day in which Eli explained to me how to break up with a girl.

Isabelle was sitting in the porch rocker wearing skinny jeans with a hole in one knee and a floppy white shirt, and she was crying in little sobs, like she'd been crying for a long time and was tired of it but couldn't stop. Her nose was pink, but she still looked beautiful anyway.

"What's the matter?" I said.

Isabelle held out Simon Dewitt Paxton's e-mail, which was crumpled up and damp.

"Read that," she said. "I actually printed it out. I was thinking I would make this scrapbook of rejections. Boyfriends I've been dumped by, colleges that turn down my applications, scholarships I don't get. Recitals I bomb in. Plays where I forget my lines. A collection of hideous failures."

She put her head down on her floppy sleeve and began to cry again, harder.

I didn't know what to do, so I read Simon Dewitt Paxton's e-mail.

TO: moonelves411
FROM: sdp526

Dear Izzy,

It's really hard to tell you this, but I know we promised always to be open and truthful to each other, and I know once you've finished reading this, you'll really be happy for me. I'm in love. Her name is Andrée, and I know I've mentioned her before. Since I'm living with her family, we've seen a lot of each other, though at first we thought we were just good friends. But suddenly this last week we discovered that we were a lot more than that. All this time she's been feeling about me just the way I've been feeling about her. Andrée said I should write right off and tell you so. So now I am.

I know now that you and I should never have thought of tying ourselves down the way we did. I know there's someone out there for you, just as perfect as Andrée is for me, and I'm glad that now you have a chance to find him.

I hope you are having a very enjoyable summer and that we will always be friends.

SDP

"SDP?" I said. "*SDP?* This guy signs a breakup letter with his *initials*?"

Which probably wasn't a tactful thing to say, but come on.

Anyway, it helped because it got Isabelle thinking of other people who went by their initials, like FDR and JFK and MLK, and she decided Simon had no business going by initials, since he wasn't nearly as good as any of them.

So then I said, why didn't we walk over to

Scrubgrass Creek, because it was a beautiful day and getting out might make her feel better.

"All right," Isabelle said. "If you don't mind a tragic companion."

"A tragic companion is okay," I said.

The twins wanted to come too, but Isabelle said no, because she couldn't stand any analogies just then.

We went down the Sowers driveway and past the pedestals, and turned right on the Fairfield Road, that was all dry and dusty, with the ditches grown up with blue chicory and yellow dandelions. Then we crossed the road and went left onto Scrubgrass Creek Road, which isn't as much a road as a track, with potholes and rocks and grass growing up in the middle. It was cooler on the creek road because it was shady, with all the trees, though there were sunny patches too, with wild daisies and red clover.

Then Isabelle took my hand. She just reached over and wrapped her hand around mine, and I felt like my heart was going to explode. Her hand felt thin and cool and elegant, like the rest of her, and in contrast my hand felt like a ham, all sweaty and hot, but Isabelle didn't seem to mind.

When we got to the bridge, we stopped in the middle and leaned on the splintery rail and looked down into the water. The creek was running fast and clear, with the sunlight sparkling off it in little golden blobs. In the dark under the bridge, you could see flickering shapes of fish, darting all together, then stopping, then darting in another direction. I've always wondered how fish knew to do that.

"Which do you think you'd be, if you were an element?" Isabelle said. "Water, fire, earth, or air?"

"I don't know," I said. I didn't have the foggiest.

"You can tell by which one makes you feel tran-scendent," Isabelle said. "You know. Whatever makes you feel dreamy and peaceful and magical. Is it watching ripples on a river or waves at the beach? Or is it gazing into a crackling fire or looking up at tow-ering mountain peaks or running with the wind?"

"Which are you?" I said.

"Oh, definitely water," Isabelle said. "If I could, I'd be a naiad, all bright and quick and glittering, with necklaces of mother-of-pearl and water lilies in my long green hair."

I thought how I felt with the wind in my face, riding my bike down Turkey Hill.

"I guess I'd be air," I said.

"You'd have wings," Isabelle said, and she turned her head and looked at me with those blue, blue eyes that felt like falling into the sky. "I could see you with wings, Danny."

And for a crazy minute I could see me with wings too, a flying boy. Zapping through the sky with Isabelle in my arms, like Superman with Lois Lane.

Isabelle bent her head and reached behind her neck and fumbled with a catch. When she straightened up, she had a necklace in her hand, the one with the broken half of a little gold heart on a thin gold chain.

"Simon has the other half," she said. "Or anyway, he did. They're supposed to fit together to make a whole. To remind us that when we were apart, we were only half a person without the other."

She paused, looking down on it.

"His is probably in some trash bin at the Louvre," she said.

I tried not to look too glad that SDP was a moron.

"I can't imagine you ever being half a person," I said.

Isabelle climbed up on the lowest rung of the bridge railing and dangled the necklace out over the water. "I'm thinking of Rose, the girl in *Titanic*," she said. "How the man she loved died when the ship went down, and it was so heartbreaking. But then afterward she escaped from her horrible fiancé and lived a long and happy life, and at the very end she threw his hateful gift of a fabulous blue diamond into the ocean."

"She should have pawned his hateful gift of a fabulous blue diamond and bought a yacht and a Ferrari," I said. "And maybe saved the homeless and cured AIDS."

"It was a grand romantic gesture," Isabelle said. "It was a repudiation of false love and all that it means."

She leaned farther over the water.

"Now I too drown false love," she said.

And she threw the necklace hard. It spun through the air, a little streak of gold, and vanished into the creek with a tiny splash.

"Some mermaid will find it," Isabelle said. "I only hope it doesn't bring her bad luck."

"She'll be all right," I said. "Unless she's a French mermaid."

Isabelle looked glum.

"I was thinking how I should have done things differently," she said. "I should have gone to visit him. Then I thought, no, maybe it's best to find out now that it wasn't meant to be."

"Sometimes it doesn't matter what you do," I said. "Sometimes things are just beyond your control. Like that iceberg rearing up in front of the *Titanic*."

"Andrée was the iceberg that sank my ship," Isabelle said tragically.

"But you're a survivor," I said. "Now you go on and live a long and happy life."

"My life sucks," Isabelle said.

But she sounded better.

We found some wild strawberries and we picked them and ate them. Then I took off my sneakers and Isabelle kicked off her flip-flops and we went wading in the creek and collected all these shiny little pebbles that looked all polished and jewel-like where the water was running over them, that Isabelle wanted to take home. We picked flowers and Isabelle made a daisy chain and put it in her hair like a crown. Then she made one for me too, and I kept it on, even though one of the stems hung down and kept tickling my ear.

"Let's never go back," Isabelle said. "Let's stay here forever and eat strawberries and live in a hollow tree."

I couldn't think of anything I'd rather do than stay on Scrubgrass Creek forever with Isabelle.

"Maybe squirrels will bring us nuts," I said. "Maybe the Moon Elves will visit."

"We can catch fish for breakfast and make dandelion wine," said Isabelle. "In the winter, we'll fly south with the birds."

"We'll probably have to," I said. "It gets pretty cold here in winter."

We lay on our backs in the grass at the edge of the water, and sometimes we talked and sometimes we didn't say anything at all, and either way it felt fine.

I thought how now this place was special to me and Isabelle, and how maybe we'd come back here again and again, year after year. Maybe we'd bring a picnic and a bottle of wine and celebrate our anniversaries, the way my mom and dad used to do at Bev's Caf.

By then the sun had dried all our pebbles out and they'd turned dull and drab, so we put them back in the creek again.

On the way home, Isabelle suddenly stopped in the middle of Scrubgrass Creek Road and put a hand on either side of my face and pulled me toward her and kissed me on the mouth. I thought I would die right there. I could feel her hands, thin and cool on my face, which by then was way hot. She smelled like clean sheets and just-cut grass, and she tasted like strawberries and sun.

"Thank you, Danny, darling," Isabelle said. "This was wonderful. You saved my life."

And we held hands again all the way back to the Sowers driveway.

That was my most perfect day. That day was pure gold.

CHAPTER 15

MARCUS JUNIUS BRUTUS (85–42 BCE)
Suicide.

··

Daniel (E.) Anderson's Book of the Dead

Then there was the party.

I had to go. It was at Ryan Baker's, and they were having a barbecue. Any other time, I would have thought it was great, because Ryan's mother makes this delicious homemade barbecue sauce and the Bakers have a swimming pool. And I've known Ryan since kindergarten.

At kindergarten graduation, Ryan and I had to do a duet of "I'm a Little Teapot," which my parents have on videotape, including a voice-over from Eli in which he says he has to leave the auditorium for a minute due to laughing so hard that he is worried about peeing his pants. After that, Eli used to call

me Teapot all the time, until we came to an agree-
ment because I threatened to kill him with Dad's
staple gun.

Usually I am a social person. Walter says that
there are seven different kinds of intelligence, one
of which is interpersonal intelligence, which means
you're good at getting along with other people.
Walter is pretty much of a moron there, though
he has so much linguistic intelligence and logical-
mathematical intelligence and visual-spatial intelligence that it probably doesn't matter. I mean, I bet
nobody ever cared if Einstein told good jokes at
parties or was friendly on teams.

But I'm like my mom that way, or at least like
the way my mom used to be. She always had lots
of friends and liked having people over to visit.
She used to have what she called rainy-day parties,
where when the weather was crappy on a Saturday,
she'd just call a lot of people up, and we'd all play
board games and eat chili she used to cook up on the
stove in this big blue pot. On our Monopoly game,
Broadway and Park Place are still sort of orange from

where Eli went bankrupt and spilled his chili bowl in despair.

That's why my mom was such a good teacher, because she just understood people and liked being around them. At the end of the school year, all her kindergartners used to cry because they didn't want to leave her and go across the hall to Ms. McKenzie, who taught first grade. Every September there were always a couple of ex-kindergartners who'd come to my mom's room anyway, and she'd have to reason with them and talk to them about new experiences and moving on, though I think what really eventually convinced them was that Ms. McKenzie's room has gerbils.

Peter Reilly was all pumped about the party. He and Amanda were going steady now, which meant that they spent their time draped all over each other in public and walking around with their hands in each other's back pockets, and Peter suddenly knew more than I would ever have believed possible about girls' underwear.

"Yvonne's going to be there too," Peter said. "She's

been kind of hanging around with Ron Mazzola, but Amanda says she's really not that into him. She still likes you. So get in there, Anderson, and make your move."

Ron Mazzola was a year ahead of us in school and was known as the Oil Man, both because of his last name and because of this gel stuff he puts on his hair. I thought that Yvonne and Ron were probably a good pair, seeing as they both had a kind of thing for strange hair. Also I didn't want to make a move on blue Yvonne. What I wanted was to be with Isabelle, just the two of us again, like that day at Scrubgrass Creek.

"Hey, I've really been talking you up," Peter said. "And so has Amanda. Look, Dan, we're supposed to do stuff *together*, right? We're best friends, right?"

"Sure," I said.

"So just *ask* her," Peter said.

"I just don't feel like it right now," I said.

"Christ, Anderson," Peter said.

And he hung up.

For a minute or so, I thought about what it would

be like to take Isabelle to Ryan's party, and how great it would feel to walk in with this really beautiful girl, and everybody envying me, and Peter Reilly with his eyes bugging out, punching me in the arm and saying *"Way to go, man."* But I knew I couldn't. It wasn't that I was ashamed of my friends. I just knew they wouldn't fit with Isabelle.

The party was on Saturday. Walter says that Einstein's theory of relativity is difficult to understand, but for a change, it's one of the few things that make perfect sense to me. Relativity means that when you can't wait for something to happen, time moves slower than a snail, and when you'd rather something never happened, ever, time shoots forward faster than a greased jackrabbit.

Which last is what time did leading up to Ryan's party. Just like that, it was Friday night, and then, before I was done worrying about it being Friday night, it was Saturday morning, and then, before I'd even begun to deal with it being Saturday morning, it was two o'clock on Saturday afternoon, and my dad was dropping me off in the Bakers' driveway and saying hi to Ryan's mother and that yes, thanks, my mom was fine, just a little tired was all, and then telling me to have a good time, and driving off, leaving me standing there with my swim trunks and a towel and a sense of impending doom.

Actually, the party started out okay. It was a great day, hot like it gets in August but not so sticky hot that you feel like you can't breathe, and Ryan's folks have this bug-zapper thing, so there weren't a zillion mosquitoes and blackflies. All the bugs fly into the zapper and get charbroiled. Every few seconds, on top of the party music, there'd be this *zzz* noise that was some bug getting fried. There was a big cooler full of drinks, and Ryan's weird uncles were all off in the yard at the barbecue grill, cooking up hot dogs and hamburgers and drinking beer.

Most of the kids were horsing around in the pool, including Ryan's little sisters and a couple of their shrimp friends who were paddling around in the shallow end with a big rubber turtle. They all yelled,

"Danny! Danny! Hi, Danny!" and started jumping up and down when they saw me, because I am good with little kids, and I thought how great it would be someday if Isabelle and I had a whole lot of little kids and lived in the old Sowers place. Though without the twins. I thought maybe we could encourage the twins to join the Peace Corps and go dig wells in someplace like Malawi.

Amanda and Yvonne were lying next to the pool on these plastic lounge chairs. Yvonne was wearing little shorts and big blue sunglasses that matched her blue hair, and Amanda was in a bikini that really had its work cut out, since up top it was about the size of a pair of gingersnaps. They waved when they saw me, and I waved back, but I didn't go over right then.

Instead I went and said hello to Ryan's weird uncles. Uncle Bug said, "Dan, how's my man?" and Uncle Rat asked if I wanted a hot dog but said to forget about the hamburgers, because Uncle Chop's unprintable son-of-an-unprintable dog had grabbed them off the plate and eaten them. Uncle Chop said to lay off his dog. He said that his dog was one good dog, and if you're going to wave a plate of hamburgers in front of a dog, well, the dog's going to eat it, because that's dog nature, and what's human nature, when there's a dog around, is to put the plate of hamburgers up where the dog can't reach it, unless the human doesn't have a brain in his pinhead because he's too busy ogling some teenage girl's backside.

That seemed to be a good time to excuse myself, so I did.

Then I changed into my swim trunks and did cannonballs into the pool, along with Ryan and Mickey Roberts and Peter and a couple of other guys, and the girls came by and sat, and kicked their feet in the water, and Yvonne talked the whole time to somebody on her pink cell phone. I hoped it was Ron the Oil Man.

So then we swam awhile and then we toweled off, and I had some lemonade and Mickey Roberts chugged two cans of soda and made himself burp, which hasn't been funny since he learned how to do it in second grade, and actually wasn't very funny even then. But we all laughed anyway, except Peter.

I was beginning to notice that Peter was ticked off.

First I thought maybe he'd had a fight with Amanda, but then I knew that was wrong because they were still all hugging, which everybody kept watching them do, hoping that Amanda's stressed-out bikini top would fall off. And then I thought maybe he was just in a lousy mood, due to his parents getting on his case or his brother Tony telling him off, which always made him what my dad calls cross as a bear with a boil on its ass. But then it became pretty clear that what was really bugging him was me. He was punching people in the arm the way he does, but not me, and when he talked to me at all, which wasn't much, he made it sound sort of nasty.

Then blue Yvonne said, "So what have you been

doing all summer, Danny? You're never around anymore."

And before I could say anything, Peter said, "He's working for that crackhead with the potatoes."

"Jim's not a crackhead," I said.

"And I'll tell you who else he's been hanging with all summer," Peter said.

And the way he said it, you could tell he was building for a fight.

"Wally the Living Dead, that's who. And the *pro-fes-sor* that's renting the Sowers house. Those are his best friends now. What do you do, Anderson, sit around all day together, reading *Play-Doh*?"

"Oh, stop it, Peter," Amanda said.

"I think the weird's rubbing off on him," Peter said. "I think over the summer he's gone weird. You guys smell anything? You guys think he's starting to smell a little weird?"

Woo-oo-oo, somebody said, and Amanda kind of giggled.

And that's when I did a rotten chicken-ass thing.

"Come off it, Reilly," I said. "The only things that smell around here are your flat feet. And I'm not hanging out with weird Wally the Living Dead. I wouldn't get near that guy with a ten-foot pole. I'm not that hard up for friends."

That's what I said.

I was like Brutus, Julius Caesar's best friend, who betrayed him and then helped stab him to death.

I was scum.

CHAPTER 16

AKASHI GIDAYU (d. 1582)
Seppuku.
....
Daniel (E.) Anderson's Book of the Dead

The party was on a Saturday, and on Monday Emma came out to the blue-potato field where I was hoeing and asked what in Sam Hill was wrong with me, because I looked like somebody just ran over my puppy.

"I'm fine," I said. Considering that I was scum.

Brutus, after stabbing Caesar, felt so rotten and guilty that he committed suicide. I wasn't that bad off, but I could see how Brutus felt.

"Yeah, sure," said Emma. "Look at the face on you. If that's fine, then I'm a whistling teakettle. Come sit down and tell me what's wrong."

I don't know what it is with Emma, the way she gets people to talk to her, but whatever it is, she'd be a hotshot if she ever got hired by the FBI or the CIA. They'd just have to put her in a room with some suspect, and in maybe thirty minutes she'd get his signed confession, along with a heartfelt apology and his whole life story from childhood pets on up. I think she's psychic. Walter says she just has a high quotient of interpersonal intelligence, but a more intense and directed kind than mine.

Also, of course, as long as you're talking to Emma, you can't be drinking her black-carrot smoothies, because it is impossible to talk and swallow at the same time, which is a point in favor of prolonged talking.

So we sat down under a tree, and I told Emma about the party and blue Yvonne and Peter Reilly and Walter and what a chicken-ass coward I was and the scum stuff I'd said.

Eli always had all these ideas for what I should do after I'd been scum. Like the time I broke the head off Angie Cook's Barbie doll at her birthday party and threw it at her, and Angie's mom called my mom and had her come take me home before the cake, Eli got all this information off the Internet for me about how to join the French Foreign Legion. And when I accidentally smashed my grandma O'Brian's Mother's Day rosebush by riding my bicycle over it, he got me a travel itinerary to Zanzibar.

But I'd done other scum stuff too. I started a fire once, back behind the barn, with some firecrackers and a leftover can of gasoline. It was a pretty big fire. It didn't go anywhere much, but it could have. I stuffed the scarf Aunt Wendy knitted for me one Christmas into the garbage can and then lied about it and said I'd lost it. I skipped school and forged my mom's name on the excuse note. I gave my cousin Georgie, who's a year younger than me, a bloody nose, just because he wanted to play Ping-Pong and wouldn't shut up and leave me alone.

Emma said my list of rotten stuff was pathetic. She said that on hers, the top five were so unspeakable, she wouldn't even tell me. Among the others were stealing twenty dollars out of her auntie Dell's pocketbook, breaking a window in the basement of the Saint John the Evangelist Catholic church, and swiping a car that belonged to one of her mom's boyfriends and smashing it into a telephone pole.

"Yeah, but you were never a traitor to a friend," I said.

Emma said she'd done a lot of mean talking behind people's backs, which was close.

"Back when I was still in school," Emma said, "there was this girl in my class, Jenny Monroe, and I just wouldn't leave her alone. She had these great clothes, designer jeans and nice boots and a leather jacket, and this great haircut, and everybody just *loved* her. I couldn't stand her, and I was mean as a snake. I said everybody knew she was nothing but a fat cow. I said her boyfriend was cheating on her with her best friend."

"What did she do?" I said.

"Nothing," said Emma. "She didn't give a hoot. I just gave her and all her cute friends a good laugh."

Because Jenny Monroe was popular, I thought.

Of course it didn't make any difference to her. But it would make a difference to Walter. Walter trusted me. Walter would feel like I'd stabbed him in the back.

Then I thought what it would be like not to be friends with Walter anymore. I thought about all the stuff Walter knows and how he made me think about things in different ways and how he always acted like what I was thinking wasn't just dumb. And how he uses his brains in a kind way, like he did with the Ouija board when he saw how freaked I was.

"You know what a real friend is?" I asked Emma.

Emma said she had an idea but she'd like to hear mine.

"A real friend is someone who likes you for who you want to be and not for who they want you to be," I said.

Emma said I had a good point, even though that sentence had a lot of *who*s.

"So what do I do now?" I said. Thinking that if Eli were around, he'd probably be on the Internet, looking up time travel for me. Or maybe seppuku.

Emma patted my knee.

"Look, Danny, your friend won't be hearing about anything from those other boys," Emma said. "You said they don't even talk to him. So if I was you, I'd let sleeping dogs lie. You just swallow it down this time and make sure you never do it again."

"I won't," I said. And I felt better.

I still felt like scum, but I felt like more optimistic scum.

And I couldn't say so, because of sounding mushy, but I can tell you that Emma's worth about a million Jenny Monroes.

Walter and Isabelle and I still got together most evenings on Isabelle's porch, and we'd talk and sometimes we'd play badminton, since the professor had put up a net in the yard, with me and Isabelle against Walter and the twins or Walter and Isabelle against me and the twins, with whoever got the twins starting out with extra points, because the twins were pretty erratic when it came to rackets and shuttlecocks. I loved that, those late-summer afternoons, with our shadows all huge across the grass, and us jumping and running, and that *tock* noise when a shuttlecock hits a racket just right, and the sun gone butter-colored, and all of us laughing and yelling.

Or if it was rainy, we'd make popcorn in the microwave and sit around watching old movies on Isabelle's parents' very small TV.

Isabelle didn't mention Simon Dewitt Paxton again, and Journey told me that she'd taken his picture out of the frame beside her bed and torn it into little pieces and flushed them down the Sowerses' mahogany toilet, which took a lot of flushes because the Sowerses' bathrooms only have those old-fashioned commodes with a tank up on the wall and a pull chain.

And I kept thinking how great it would be if Isabelle didn't have to leave at the end of the summer but just stayed on at the Sowers house, with her mother painting orange cows and her dad maybe teaching his history at the community college over in Johnson City, which is the next town past Fairfield but is a lot bigger, with a shopping mall. I'd tell

Isabelle how I felt about her, and she'd realize she felt the same way about me too, and she'd talk her parents around, because nobody could resist Isabelle. Maybe when my mom met Isabelle, she'd get interested in things again, and my dad would see that with a girl like Isabelle, I had a future after all.

Men make plans and the mice in the ceiling laugh.

CHAPTER 17

MR. JONAS H. PILCHER (1916–2003)
Died of emphysema.

BERNIE THE DOG (1990–2003)
Died of a broken heart.

Daniel (E.) Anderson's Book of the Dead

The problem with letting sleeping dogs lie, like Emma said, is that they don't stay lying down. You know what dogs are like. There they all are, flopped out flat on the porch like a bunch of fur pancakes, snoring up a storm, but when you try to sneak past, even creeping along on tiptoe and holding your breath, in like two seconds they're all riled up and jumping around and barking their fool heads off.

Though of course my sleeping dogs might have stayed asleep a little longer if it hadn't been for bad luck, bad timing, the green bus, and the twins. With my sleeping dogs, it was like I put on football cleats and stomped on their tails.

The green bus belongs to Henry Jones, who was the oldest friend of old Mr. Pilcher, Jim Pilcher's grandfather. When old Mr. Pilcher died, Henry Jones was so sad over it that he was drunk for two straight weeks. He just sat on his porch in his undershirt and pajama bottoms and drank rye whiskey out of the bottle and cried. Then he sobered up and said he was done with his period of mourning and it was time for him to move on. Then he went over to Springfield and bought himself a secondhand school bus. His wife said that grief had deranged his mind.

It wasn't a big full-size school bus. It was one of those little ones, like they use for the special kids and the preschoolers in the Head Start program. Henry Jones painted it green, and in good weather he'd drive it around all the country roads and pick people up and take them into Fairfield, and then later he'd collect them and bring them all home again. He charged two bucks a person, round-trip, except for kids under five, who were free. Lots of people rode the green bus, because it was environmentally better than everybody driving all the time in separate cars and enriching the big oil companies. Also it was friendly. Also it was a way of getting to town if you weren't old enough to drive and your dad said he had better things to do than ferry you around, and what did you think he was, a goddamn chauffeur?

So one day along the middle of August, I rode the green bus into town as part of my job, to order chicken wire and four yards of mulch for the blue-potato farm and to pick up prenatal vitamin pills for Emma, which was an aside. The twins came along too, because they were going to the library in hopes of finding out how to make nitroglycerin. They were both wearing T-shirts and jeans. Journey's shirt was covered with little rhinestone hearts, and Jasper's said GOOD MORNING — I SEE THE ASSASSINS HAVE FAILED.

Also on the bus were Henry Jones's friend Clarence Carmichael, who always went along for the ride to keep Henry Jones company, and the entire membership of the Fairfield Women's Book Club and

Coffee Circle, who were going to Bev's Caf to drink coffee and discuss *Othello*, Evelyn Perry's divorce, and pasta recipes.

Back before Eli died, my mom belonged to the Fairfield Women's Book Club and Coffee Circle. She used to like it a lot, particularly on the last Friday of every month, when it turned into the Fairfield Women's Movie Club and Wine Bar and they met at different people's houses to watch chick flicks and do manicures. They'd come home all giggly, with funny-colored fingernails, smelling like cabernet and popcorn and acetone. I thought of my mom now, just lying there alone at home, and I wished she were back in the Movie Club and Wine Bar. I thought if she'd just be that way again, I wouldn't make fun of her purple fingernails, and I'd even agree with her about how great Julia Roberts was in *Pretty Woman*, though I am not a Julia Roberts fan.

We all got off the bus and I walked the twins to the library. It was hotter in town. Some little kids in the park wearing nothing but underpants were jumping in and out of the fountain, while their mothers sat off under a tree. Eli said I used to go in that fountain bare naked, back when I was too young to remember. I'd always hoped he was making that up.

"So what's with the nitroglycerin?" I said.

"Jasper read about it in *The Golden Book of Chemistry,*" Journey said. "Nitroglycerin is a powerful and dangerous explosive."

"If I knew how to make it, I would win the science fair," Jasper said.

"Nobody's going to tell you how to make it," I said. "Why don't you just build paper airplanes or something, like everybody else?"

"Because I am exceptionally intelligent," Jasper said. "I need a challenge."

After I dropped off the twins, I went all the way to the east end of Main Street to Fournier's Farm Supply and ordered chicken wire and mulch like Jim told me, and then I trudged all the way back to the west end of Main Street to Whitman's Drugstore for Emma's vitamin pills, by which time I felt like a desert explorer dying of sunstroke. When I passed the library for the second time, the twins were sitting on the front steps, looking dismal and forlorn due to not having found any instruction manuals on the manufacture of death-dealing explosives. Instead, the children's librarian had collared them and made them check out a copy of *The Wind in the Willows.* She said they could learn a lot from studying the reckless character of Toad.

"If I were in *The Wind in the Willows,* I would not be the reckless character of Toad," Jasper said bitterly.

"You would both be the reckless character of Toad," I said. "Let's go to Bev's Caf and get some ice cream."

I figured ice cream should make up for them being deprived of the opportunity to blow up the county, or at least the Sowers carriage house. Also it was really hot.

Bev's Caf has little tables with umbrellas on the sidewalk where you can sit outside in summer, but those were all full of people with shopping bags having iced tea and a guy with a briefcase doing the crossword puzzle on the back page of the newspaper and Henry Jones and Clarence Carmichael having lemonade and arguing about Chevrolets.

"There's Walter!" Journey said.

"Where?" I said.

"Right there!" Journey said, pointing. "See? Hey! Hey, Walter!"

And there was Walter, sitting in Bev's window and having a Coke, which usually wasn't the sort of thing Walter would do, except it turned out later that he'd come into town on the green bus too, only earlier, because his mother had called from work to say that she'd forgotten her wallet, and then he'd brought her the wallet, and then he'd gone to the library, only before the twins, and now there he was, sitting in Bev's Caf and waiting for the green bus to take him home.

"Hey, Walter!" Journey yelled, jumping all around and waving.

Walter looked up and saw us and gave us a sort of funny little smile.

"I bet *he* knows how to make nitroglycerin," Jasper said.

"I bet he won't tell you," I said. "Now shut up about it unless you want to spend the rest of your life being escorted to the bathroom by a social worker."

The twins went racketing up the steps and into the Caf, with me following along with my bagful of prenatal vitamins.

Bev's Caf isn't fancy, but it's nice. There are booths along the wall, upholstered in some stuff that looks like leather but is more resistant to spills, and tables with flowered tablecloths in the middle of the floor, which were all shoved together just then for the Women's Book Club and Coffee Circle, and a lot of photos on the wall of all the people Bev likes. Some of them are famous people, like Katharine Hepburn and Johnny Cash and Martin Luther King Jr. and Princess Diana, but there are pictures too of all Bev's kids and grandkids, and one of her and her husband, Roy, both a lot skinnier and wearing headbands and fringed jackets, back in 1969, the year they went to Woodstock. Eli's picture was up there too, with him wearing his football uniform and giving his crookedy grin.

"Why, hi, Danny," Bev said. "We haven't seen you in a while. How's your mom?"

"She's okay," I said, which I knew and Bev knew and I knew Bev knew was a lie. Everybody knew my mom had been kind of nuts ever since Eli died.

The twins were scrambling into the booth with Walter.

"How do you like working for Jim?" Bev said. "That going pretty good?"

"Yeah," I said.

"They're good kids, Jim and Emma," Bev said. "Jim's mom says they're having a baby. I guess she's counting on a girl, because last time she was in here, she had this great big sack full of pink yarn. You tell them I said hi, okay? And tell them not to be such a pair of strangers."

"Sure," I said.

"No," I heard Walter saying to the twins.

"You going to sit over there with your friends?" Bev said.

I looked where she was looking, which wasn't toward the twins and Walter. Peter Reilly and

Amanda were sitting in a booth across the room. Peter was wearing a T-shirt with the sleeves torn off, and it looked like his biceps had gotten even bigger over the summer, what with hauling all those boards and cement blocks around. Amanda was wearing a strapless sundress, and it looked like parts of her had gotten bigger too. I hadn't talked to Peter since Ryan Baker's party, but he waved me on over anyway.

"Have a seat, Anderson," Peter said.

I looked over at Walter and the twins. Walter was staring down into his Coke like he was sighting sea cucumbers at the bottom of the Mariana Trench. I knew he'd just told the twins to pipe down and leave me alone, because Jasper was saying, "*Why* do we have to pipe down and leave him alone?" and Journey was saying, "Isn't he going to sit with us? He said we'd get ice cream."

Tell the twins: tell the world.

"Or are you *too busy*?" Peter said. "Or do you need to go read some *Play-Doh*? What's with you, Anderson? Am I smelling weird?"

"Oh, stop it, Peter," Amanda said.

Walter hadn't taken his eyes off that Coke. Like if he didn't watch it, the Loch Ness monster or something might jump out of it.

Then I knew that Walter telling the twins to leave me alone was like giving me the go-ahead to sit with Peter and Amanda. He was telling me it was all right to pretend he wasn't there. And I thought how easy it would be to just pretend and go ahead and sit down.

And right off I started rationalizing how it was okay really, how Walter wouldn't mind. I could make it up with Walter later. Peter Reilly and I would still be friends, and I'd still sit on the back seat of the bus, and I'd still be on Peter's team. I thought how lousy I'd feel if I got off the bus and Peter and Mickey and Ryan and all were going *whoo-oo-oo* together and laughing and flicking jelly beans at me.

Then I thought how I'd promised Emma I'd quit being scum and how back when I was eight and under the dining-room table, Eli had said never to wimp out on a real friend. For a minute I thought about my pirate ship, which I hadn't thought about in years. I wondered if there were still pirates out there and how you got to be one. Right now seemed like a good time to run away to sea.

But instead I said, "Come on, Reilly, give it a rest. That Play-Doh thing isn't funny anymore."

Which doesn't sound like much as life-changing statements go, but then when you think about it, a lot of life-changing statements probably aren't very grand. Like how Rosa Parks wouldn't get up out of her seat on the bus. What I bet she said was something like "I'm staying right here; my feet are tired." And then the whole civil rights movement started.

Not that my statement was as life-changing as hers. But it was a lot for me.

Then I thought, *This is dumb to get in a fight over.*

So I said, "Hey, why don't you guys come over and sit with us?"

"No, thanks," Peter said.

Then he said, "You sit with whoever you want, Anderson. You hang out with any weirdo you want to. I could give a rat's ass. But don't try crawling back later. I don't do weird."

And when I just stood there, thinking what to say

next, he said, "Go on, get the hell away from me," and he grabbed a bunch of those sugar packets that Bev keeps in little bowls on the tables and threw them at my face. So I grabbed him by the T-shirt and he jumped out of the booth and we started punching each other back and forth and Amanda started screeching. Walter told me later that the twins were trying to stab Peter in the kidneys with a couple of Bev's forks, but he nabbed them in time. Then Bev's son, Arnold, who's built like a tank, came out of the kitchen and threw us all out, but not before I got a black eye.

Walter says this isn't because Peter hates me all of a sudden. Peter acts that way because he needs to be in control of stuff because he's insecure.

But for whatever reason, that fight pretty much ended life as I'd known it.

I wasn't in anymore. I was jelly-bean bait.

CHAPTER 18

HERNÁN CORTÉS (1485–1547)
Died of pleurisy.
....
Daniel (E.) Anderson's Book of the Dead

Here's my question: Is there free will? Do we decide things for ourselves? Or is everything all preprogrammed and we just toddle along down the track, sometimes falling into stuff by mistake like those cartoon characters falling down manholes?

I guess what started me thinking about this was when Walter told me about the Butterfly of Doom. The Butterfly of Doom is why you can't go back in time and fix your life and make everything come out better.

The butterfly comes from this quote that says a butterfly flapping its wings in New Hampshire can set off a typhoon in the China Sea. The butterfly flap makes some tiny little change that causes another tiny little change that causes another and another, and it all keeps multiplying until finally you've got palm trees snapping all over Indonesia and you're in the middle of a typhoon. But if you went back in time to try to stop the typhoon, you couldn't, because you'd never find the butterfly.

The butterfly thing really creeps me out, to tell you the truth. It's like you don't eat your Cheerios one morning and just because of that, forty years later a grand piano falls on your head. Somewhere maybe there was some tiny little thing Eli did that set him on the way to his roadside bomb. That's chaos theory, Walter says.

Which only confirms my belief that the worst thing that ever happened to the human race is math.

Isabelle was leaving on the last day of August.

I had it marked on the calendar on the back of my bedroom door. The calendar came from Ernie's Bait and Tackle, and every month had a picture of a fish. The August fish was this really mournful-looking largemouth bass. Every day I'd cross off a day, and

213

it would be that much closer to Isabelle going away, and that fish would just look at me like it knew how I felt. That bass was one sad fish.

I still had all these plans for how I'd persuade Isabelle not to leave, how I'd get her to stay, and I'd play them over and over like little movies in my mind. I'd tell her I loved her, and suddenly she'd see me like for the very first time, and then we'd fall into each other's arms and the music would come up and there'd be this really gorgeous sunset.

We'd pledge ourselves to each other, like she and Simon Dewitt Paxton did, only this time it would be forever and for real. Even if she had to go back to New York for a while, because of her father's job, we'd write to each other every day, because Isabelle thinks letters are more romantic than e-mails, and I could see myself at our dented-up mailbox, getting her letters in the mail, all in her swoopy red handwriting. "Darling Danny," they'd begin, and they'd end, "Love always, Isabelle."

Then, maybe after we graduated from high school, she'd come back and I'd build a little house for us over at the blue-potato farm. I'd plant a garden for her with roses and daisies, and we'd have a little porch where we could watch the full moon and the fireflies.

"They're magic," Isabelle would say, looking at the fireflies. And I'd reach out and take her hand and say, "No, that's you."

That's the kind of stuff I thought about. I'd lie awake at night making plans, each one dumber than the last.

The days on the calendar kept filling up with X's. It was five days, then three days, then two days. Then it was hours.

And it wasn't anything like I'd planned.

On that last night, we were all there, me and Isabelle and Walter and the twins, on the old Sowers porch. It was still summer, but you could tell summer was over really, done with us, on its way out. You can always tell. The light changes and there's this feel to the air.

The twins were all droopy and subdued, sitting close to each other on the porch steps and speaking only when spoken to, which was weird, since getting them to shut up would ordinarily take a sledgehammer or one of those drugs that the wildlife guys use to down rogue elephants. Jasper was wearing a T-shirt that said HOPE IS FOR SISSIES. Journey's shirt said I HATE PEOPLE.

Walter looked like the fish on my calendar, and I probably looked worse. But Isabelle was all lit up and kept talking faster and faster about all the marvelous things there were to do back home and all the marvelous places she'd take us when we came to visit.

Suddenly *marvelous* was one of Isabelle's words.

"You'll love it, darlings," she said over and over. About the Guggenheim, the Met, the Cloisters, the Russian Tea Room, Times Square. The lions, Patience and Fortitude, in front of the New York Public Library.

I thought Patience and Fortitude were lousy names for lions. Lions should have more active names, like Simba and Leo.

"Did you know the Harry Potter books are over?"

Journey said mournfully. "This summer was the very last Harry Potter book."

"Journey was sad when Voldemort died," Jasper said. "If Journey was a Harry Potter character, she would be Voldemort."

"Nobody liked Voldemort," I said.

"I did," Journey said.

"Do you think you'll be back again next summer?" Walter said.

Say yes, I thought.

But Isabelle just shrugged and shook out her silky hair.

"Who knows where we'll be next summer?" Isabelle said. "Anything could happen. Maybe we'll meet next in some foreign city, where there are temple bells and palm trees and the air smells of cinnamon."

"If Jasper was a city," Journey said, "he would be Detroit."

And I knew right then that it was over. We'd never go to visit, and we'd never meet in a foreign city full of temple bells, and Isabelle wasn't coming back. She was trying to patch it over with all the *marvelous* talk, but I knew she was done forever with Fairfield and with Walter and with me. She was leaving us behind, going back to the symphony and the art museum and her fancy private school. Her father the professor had finished his monograph, and her mother was done with painting boxy orange cows. It was over, and I was too old to go back to Neverland.

Everything I'd imagined about Isabelle and me was just dumb.

"*We're* coming back," Journey said. "Jasper and I buried a time capsule behind the carriage house, and we're coming back to dig it up. We're coming back in twelve years, when we're twenty-one. Will you still be here when we're twenty-one?"

Probably, I thought.

"It's romantic, really, being forcibly torn asunder like this in our youth," Isabelle said. "We should send a token each year to show that in spite of everything, we'll always be true. A single red rose, like in *The Prisoner of Zenda*."

"You could just post on your Facebook page," Jasper said.

Then we sat there not saying anything much, because there really wasn't anything left to say, just watching the fireflies blink off and on in the tall grass. I had a pain in my chest that felt like my heart was going to explode. *This is what a broken heart feels like*, I thought. *My heart is blowing up like a Japanese octopus trap and I'm going to die and the last thing I'll see will be Isabelle with the stars behind her, looking like fireflies in her hair.*

I knew I'd never tell Isabelle how I felt about her now. It was too late, and it had always been too late or too early, or anyway just wrong. Somewhere in my past I'd picked a dandelion or something, and that was the Butterfly of Doom. Something had set me on the path to being the wrong person in the wrong place at the wrong time, to losing Isabelle, to Isabelle going away.

Then Isabelle's mother came to the door, looking tired, and said how lovely it had been for Isabelle and the twins to be friends with us this summer, but now it was really time for them all to come inside because they had an early start in the morning and they still had packing to do. Journey started to cry.

"I don't want to go home," Journey said. "I want to live here."

"Don't be silly," Isabelle said.

Then she kissed Walter and she kissed me, and she hugged me hard.

"I'll be in touch, darlings," she said. "It's been wonderful."

And then she went inside and closed the door. Walter and I just stood there for a minute. Then we went down the Sowers porch steps and headed down the driveway toward the empty Sowers pedestals and the road.

"You all right, Danny?" Walter said.

"Sure," I said.

Though I wasn't.

"Look, Dan," Walter said, "you knew she was

never going to stay. She was only sort of playing with us, really. It wasn't going to last."

"Sure, I knew that," I said.

But I hadn't, I really hadn't. I was that dumb.

I should have remembered that story from Greek mythology about what happens to boys with wings.

I should have remembered Miss Walker's poem. *Nothing gold can stay.*

When I got home, my mom was up in her bedroom, lying down with the lights off, and my dad was in the living room, watching TV, a rerun of some cop show with lots of tire noise and gunfire. I went up to my room.

Back when I was little, Eli and I watched this old movie *The Wizard of Oz.* It starts out all in black and white on this little farm in the middle of nowhere in Kansas, and then a cyclone whirls in and takes Dorothy and her dog and her whole house to Oz. When she gets to Oz, it's a magical kingdom where everything is suddenly in Technicolor, and there are witches and flying monkeys and the Emerald City.

But all Dorothy wants is to get back to black-and-white Kansas again.

I thought that was nuts, and so did Eli. He said nobody who got out of Kansas ever voluntarily went back.

That's how I felt, walking up the stairs that night to my room. Like for a whole summer I'd lived in this magical rainbow country, and now it was over. Now I was back home. *There's no place like home,* I thought. Where Peter Reilly was going to make the rest of my life a living hell. Where Eli was gone and my mom was gone and my dad had always been gone and anyway thought I was dumb as a stump.

I hated them all. I even hated Jim and Emma, because they were happy and I wasn't, and Walter, because he was going to have a successful brilliant life, and the twins, because they were too young to have any problems and didn't have the sense to see how lucky they were. I stopped in the hall in front of Eli's bedroom door. It was shut, like it always was, and the light was off inside. Downstairs a commercial came on, and I could hear my dad walking out to the kitchen to get a beer. No one was around to stop me, so I opened the door to Eli's room and turned on the overhead light and went inside. Then I locked the door behind me. And then I started to take Eli's stuff down.

I tore his posters and his brown paper down off the wall and crumpled them up and stuffed them in the wastebasket, and I tore all the sheets and blankets off the bed and threw them in the middle of the floor in a big pile. I dragged all his clothes out of the closet and yanked them off the hangers — shirts and pants and jackets and the gray suit he'd worn in his scholarship picture — and I dumped out all his bureau drawers. Then I started throwing stuff out of his desk. Papers he'd written and notebooks and pencils and pens. A bottle of ink smashed, and I threw a whole drawer after it. I threw his clock radio, and the plastic cover cracked across. I kicked at his bedside lamp, and it fell and smashed and little pieces of lightbulb skittered all over the floor.

I was crying and breathing in big sick gasps.

"Why did you have to do it?" I shouted at Eli's

empty room. "Why did you *leave*? *Why does everybody leave?*"

And I shoved at Eli's bookcase, and the whole thing teetered and fell and books spilled out.

By then my parents were outside, pounding on Eli's door, and my dad was shouting, "What the hell is going on in there? Daniel! Open this damn door!"

Eli's room looked like a cyclone had hit it. My hand was bleeding where I'd cut it on something. I stood there a minute, catching my breath. Then I climbed across the mess of stuff and opened Eli's door.

"What have you done?" my mom said, and her voice went all shaky and ragged. *"What have you done?"*

"I think you ought to see a doctor," I said to my mom. "I think how you're acting is crazy. I think you should see a psychiatrist."

I was trying not to cry.

"Eli's not here," I said. "Eli's not here anymore. But I am. *I am!*"

"Danny," my dad said.

"You leave me alone," I said. "Don't talk to me anymore. Don't talk to me ever again. Just leave me the hell alone."

And I went into my own room and slammed the door. Outside I could hear my mom crying, but I didn't care. I sat on my bed and thought about the Spanish conquistador Hernán Cortés in my Book of the Dead. There's a story that when Cortés first landed in Mexico, he burned all his ships so that he and his men would have no way to retreat.

I'd always thought that was a pretty shortsighted thing to do. Like Eli always said, it's important to have a backup plan. But then I thought, *No, Cortés was right.*

Sometimes you have to destroy the past so that you'll have to learn how to live in the new world.

CHAPTER 19

NAPOLEAN BONAPARTE (1769–1821)
Poison wallpaper.

JOSEPHINE BONAPARTE (1763–1814)
Pneumonia.

Daniel (E.) Anderson's Book of the Dead

I figured that after what I'd done to Eli's room, I'd be lucky to ever see the light of day again, or maybe I'd only see it from the barred windows of some juvenile detention facility in Saskatchewan.

But the morning afterward, when I came downstairs, my mom was already there, doing stuff with frying pans. So instead of a baloney-and-mustard sandwich, like I usually made myself for breakfast, I had cinnamon French toast. She had big purple circles under her eyes, and her hands were a little shaky, but her hair was all combed, and she had this list she'd made with a lot of names and phone numbers on a pad. And she didn't seem to blame me for going raving berserk.

"I'm so sorry, Danny," she said. "I'm so very sorry."

"I'm the one who should be sorry, not you," I said. "I'm the one that made the mess."

My mom shook her head.

"No, honey," she said. "It wasn't you."

She put a pitcher of maple syrup on the table, next to my plate of French toast.

"I used to dream about him all the time," she said. "About how he was when he was a little boy. I could see him just as clear. Then he just seemed to get further and further away, and I couldn't let him go, Danny. I just couldn't."

"Yeah, I know," I said.

My mom's voice got a little stronger, and suddenly she sounded more like I remembered my mom.

"And last night I could hear him," she said. "I swear, Danny, I could hear his voice. And you know what he said?"

"What?" I said.

My mom gave a sort of rueful little smile.

"He said, 'Come on, Mom, get a grip.'"

That day she called a bunch of doctors and found one that could see her right away. She was diagnosed with prolonged grief disorder, which is sort of like post-traumatic stress syndrome for the bereaved. Then she got some pills, and a while after that she joined a survivors' therapy group.

She must have talked to my dad too, because he never said one word to me about trashing Eli's room, which wasn't like my dad. After I finished cleaning up, he helped me carry stuff downstairs, and we took Eli's clothes to the church poor box, except for his Catamount football shirt and his lucky fishing hat, which I kept. My dad thinks that maybe he'll make an office in that room, or maybe a den with a TV.

When that was all done, he took me over to Bev's Caf for a milk shake, and he didn't talk about my grades. Though you could tell he was pretty messed up about how to begin.

"Danny, we never meant . . ." he said, and then,

"I wouldn't want you to think . . ." and then I said, "What?"

And he said, "We love you just as much as we loved Eli, Dan. We always have. It's just . . . after him going like that . . ."

And I said, "Yeah, I know." Because I really did know.

"You know I was raised on a farm," my dad said after he blew his nose. "It didn't suit me, but my dad and his — well, you come from a long line of farmers. Looks like maybe it's in your blood."

"Yeah, maybe," I said.

Then we talked about the blue-potato farm and how in a couple of years I might like to go to the state agricultural college. Then Bev came over and said we looked like men who might like another round of milk shakes, and we said sure. It wasn't a total father-son breakthrough, but it was a start.

"You still keep that dead book?" my dad asked as we walked out the door. "Or is that all done?"

"I don't know," I said.

. . .

There's an *-ology* for practically anything anybody is interested in. If you don't believe me, just ask Walter. Xenobiology is the study of aliens. Nidology is the study of birds' nests. Fromology is the study of cheese.

Thanatology is the study of death.

What I thought about right off when I first heard that was ninjas, but with academic degrees. Death-expert ninjas who could leap thirty feet in the air and take people out with a *shuriken,* like in *Crouching Tiger, Hidden Dragon.* There could be T-shirts, I thought. DON'T MESS WITH ME. I'M A THANATOLOGIST.

But it turns out that thanatology isn't about making people die. It's more about coping with it when they do. It's about closure.

Here are what Walter says are the Five Stages of Coping with Death:

Denial

Anger

Bargaining

Depression

Acceptance

The Victorians, when somebody died, wore black clothes and weeping veils for a year. They blew their noses on black-bordered handkerchiefs and they wrote their letters on black-bordered stationery. They wore jewelry made of dead people's hair. Isabelle thought that was creepy, especially the hair.

But Walter said it was a healthy transitional thing to do. "It helps people move from denial to acceptance," Walter said.

He turned to me.

"You know, Dan. Like you're doing with your Book of the Dead."

"What?" I said.

"Well, what do you think that's all about?" Walter said. "It's a book of *dead people*, Danny. What do you think you're doing that for?"

"It's just a hobby," I said.

"Yeah, right," Walter said. "It's a coping mechanism. It's desensitization therapy."

"You mean you think if I write enough about dead people, Eli being dead won't bother me anymore?" I said. Kind of angry.

Walter shrugged up his bony shoulders.

"You're coming to terms with it, Dan," he said. "That's a good thing. What you're doing with that book, you're finding closure."

"That's crap," I said.

Even Walter doesn't know everything, I thought.

But that was before I found Eli's last words.

Walter and Isabelle and I once had a talk about famous last words.

"What would your last words be?" Isabelle said. "Pretend it's your last chance to leave a message for posterity."

She flopped back dramatically on the grass and raised one hand to her brow.

"There you are in your canopy bed, pale and wan, under a red velvet cover with gold tassels. Your loved ones are weeping all around you, and you — slowly — lift your head from the pillow for the very last time. What would you say?"

Walter said uncooperatively that in his opinion you should have delivered your message to posterity well before you flopped over on your red velvet deathbed.

"Napoleon's last word was 'Josephine,'" Isabelle said. "He died with the name of the woman he truly loved on his lips. 'Josephine.' I think that's beautiful."

I thought how my last word might be "Isabelle."

Walter said, "Kit Carson's last words were 'I wish I had another bowl of chili.'"

Journey said, "When Jasper's goldfish died, he wanted to freeze it in an ice-cube tray. But instead we put it in the trash compactor."

Nobody wanted to talk about Jasper's goldfish.

"All right, would you rather fade out gracefully?" said Isabelle. "Or would you rather 'rage against the dying of the light'?"

Isabelle chose fading gracefully, Jasper and Journey picked rage, and Walter picked immortality, due to planning to have his brain circuitry copied into a computer. He says this technology will be available to everybody, possibly within the next fifty years.

I kind of sided with the twins there, because the thought of dying pisses me off. I mean, you spend a whole lifetime learning stuff and educating yourself and having ideas, and then it's all gone — *pfft!* — just like that. What kind of sense does that make?

Then I thought how Eli probably didn't have time for any last words. It's not like running over a bomb gives you much time.

But it turned out he had last words after all. I found them when I cleaned up the rest of the wreck I'd made of his room.

Way in the back of his closet, he had a stash of these really hot magazines full of naked girls. There was some other stuff back there too, like a box of condoms and a pack of Camel cigarettes and some stuff in a plastic bag that looked like oregano but wasn't. And next to all that was my old pink dragon, which did look sort of like an anteater, which goes

234

to show that 3-D visual arts aren't going to be my thing. Under the dragon was a letter in an envelope. DANNY, it said in Eli's writing, which was really more like printing, but he could do it really fast. So I sat down on the floor of the closet and opened it.

Dear Danny,

If you find this, you must be snooping through these magazines, you little turd. At least I hope it's you that finds this stuff and not Mom.

And I guess the thing is, if you're reading this at all, I'm probably not around anymore.

I really believe I'll make it through fine and that this time next year I'll be back in the US of A. I hope you'll never read this.

But if things don't work out, I hope you'll understand. Sometimes, when things go wrong, you just have to do the best you can to try to fix them. I'm not sure this war is right, Dan. But I don't want people to die who don't have to. You know how I felt when the towers went down. I wanted to be there, helping, and I wasn't. Maybe I feel like this is my second chance.

Anyway, kid, just in case, here's what I'd never tell you to your face: you're the best little brother a guy could ever have. If I'm not around to watch you grow up, I'll be really pissed.

I feel like I should give you all this advice, but now that I'm sitting here, I don't know what the hell to say.

Read Catcher in the Rye. *It's a really good book.*

Don't let any of your dumb runt friends talk you into doing anything you don't want to do.

Don't ever buy a used car from Bernie Underwood.

If I'm out of the picture, get Jim Pilcher to take you out for that first beer when you turn twenty-one. He owes me big-time for that thing with the raccoon.

Shit. I'm no good at this.

The radio's playing Sinatra. Some oldie about "All my bright tomorrows belong to you." Hell, maybe it's a sign. Well, if I don't come back, they're all yours, Dan, along with my lucky fishing hat.

I love you.

Eli

And suddenly I was crying like the little kid I'd never be again because I knew that Eli was dead, that this was the last I'd ever in this world hear from Eli.

Those were Eli's last words.

CHAPTER 20

HENRY MOSELEY (1887–1915)
Shot at the Battle of Gallipoli.

....

Daniel (E.) Anderson's Book of the Dead

I told Jim about Eli's letter, but I couldn't get Jim to tell me about the thing with the raccoon. He says he'll save it until I'm twenty-one and we've had several legal beers.

"Hey, Dan, I'm no Eli," he said. "But you need anything anytime, Emma and me, we'll be right here."

That felt pretty good to hear, and I told him so.

I told Emma about trashing Eli's room.

"You think it's going to get any better at home?" I said. "With me and my mom and dad?"

Emma was starting to get fat then with the baby, and she was drinking yogurt shakes with lots of calcium, so she made me a yogurt shake with calcium too. It was a little weird tasting but a whole lot better than those black-carrot things.

"I don't know, Danny," she said. "You want to know that, you need to ask somebody a lot smarter than me. But if I had to guess, I'd say your family's been like the Secret Garden, all shut up and dead-looking for a long time. Maybe what you did, that's what it took to get it growing again."

Next to Walter, Emma might be the smartest person I know.

The first day of school, it felt kind of strange not to sit in the back seat of the bus, like I always had before. Peter Reilly was there, horsing around and punching people in the arm the way he does, but he didn't even look at me. With Peter, once you're gone, you're gone. Just ask one of his ex–serious girlfriends.

Then the bus stopped at Cemetery Road, and Walter got on, lugging his funky old briefcase, and sat down next to me on the front seat, the one that's as far out as you can possibly get.

"Hi, Dan," Walter said, and he gave me that crookedy grin.

"Hi, Walter," I said.

Emma and Jim had a girl baby in January, and they named her Rain. They got married in the spring, just before planting time, and I was the best man. Now they're talking about baby number two.

This year I've got Miss Walker in English class, and she gave me a copy of *Walden* by Henry David Thoreau. It might just turn out to be my special book, she said. A man who spends his time making the earth say blue potatoes might hit it off with a man who made the earth say beans.

"What?" I said.

"Chapter seven," she said.

Then she assigned me an essay on it.

Being out didn't turn out to be as awful as I thought it was going to be. After a while Ryan Baker started coming over to sit with me and Walter in the cafeteria, and then we picked up a couple of girls, and then all (three) members of the rocket club, and a kid from Brazil who's a chess whiz in Portuguese.

Peter Reilly's now on his eighth serious girlfriend, and we're civil to each other.

I don't hear from Isabelle anymore. She's moved on. We all have. It's just hard that moving on sometimes means leaving people behind.

I wish I could say that I've come to terms with what happened to my brother Eli, but I haven't. I don't think I ever will. I think about how things would be different, how much he would have done if he were here. For every person killed, Walter would say, so many parallel universes get snuffed out. In my Book of the Dead, there's Henry Moseley, a British scientist who was so brilliant that everybody thought he was headed for a Nobel Prize. Instead, when he was twenty-seven, he was drafted, sent to fight in World War I, and shot through the head and killed at the Battle of Gallipoli.

After that, the British government pulled its head out of its ass and decided to stop sending all their scientists off to war. But by that time it was too late, and the world we might have had if Henry Moseley had stayed in it was long gone.

Like the world we might have had if Eli could have stuck around.

Mostly, though, I don't think about Eli dying anymore. Maybe the old Egyptians were right that dying is a journey from the world of the living to whatever comes next, and that it takes a long time. It's the same for the survivors too, and for me, my journey's done. I think that maybe all this time with my Book of the Dead, I've been building a bridge between the world with Eli in it and the world without him, and now I've crossed over and I'm on the other side. I've reached what Walter calls closure, about which I guess Walter was right after all.

I don't know where Eli is. But I can tell you this: his heart was lighter than that stupid feather. That old Egyptian Gobbler thing didn't get Eli.

Walter once told me a quote from a Roman poet named Virgil. "Death twitches my ear. *Live,* he says. *I am coming.*"

"If you're trying to make me feel better," I said, "telling me that a guy with a scythe is lurking just around the corner is not helping. You are terminally creeping me out."

Walter said no, it was a good thing. It was saying, make the most of your tomorrows, because life doesn't last forever. Eli would have said that.

Which makes me think of Jennie Wade, the girl who got killed by mistake at the Battle of Gettysburg, when a bullet came through the kitchen door while she was kneading dough. The day after she died, her mother took all that dough and baked it into bread. It made fifteen loaves of bread.

When I first heard that, I thought it was pretty heartless, just baking after your daughter died as if nothing at all had happened. But now I think it was the right thing to do.

Because life goes on and people have to eat.

In November, the November after Isabelle left, I went for one last time to visit Eli's grave. The wind was blowing out of the north, and the sky was gray and angry looking. Fall was pretty far gone. If a storm came that night, I figured it would take down the rest of the leaves.

"I'm not going to keep my Book of the Dead anymore," I said.

The wind gave a little gust like an answer, and a whole bunch of leaves blew across Eli's grave. I sat there for a long time.

I thought about how lucky I'd been to have Eli for a brother. I thought about all the stuff he'd tried to teach me. I thought of how, because of him, I had Jim and Emma and Walter and Miss Walker, and how because of him, Mom and Dad and I were working on being a family again. I thought how much I'd always miss him, and how I'd never forget him and how I'd carry his memory with me all my life.

If I ever had kids, I'd tell them about him. And I thought how I'd do my best to see that all those bright tomorrows he'd left me that should have been his didn't go to waste.

"I swear and double-swear on a two-foot stack of Bibles," I said. Like I was making a pact between Eli and me.

By the time I got up, my knees and fingers had gone stiff, and it was getting cold. I reached over and patted the top of Eli's stone, gentle, like I'd sometimes seen Coach Bowers pat a football player's shoulder after he'd played a really good game.

"Good-bye, Eli," I said. "I love you."

And then I headed home.

ACKNOWLEDGMENTS

Many thanks to Cynthia Platt, my creative and kind-hearted editor; to Mike Miller and his science class, for so neatly solving the problem of E.T.; to Ethan Rupp, for averting computer disaster; and to Mary Lee Donovan and all of the wonderful people at Candlewick who make books possible.

MORE STORIES ABOUT LIFE AND FAMILY
FROM REBECCA RUPP

★ "An unsettling, thought-provoking, and sensitive exploration of the intersections of faith, work, and family."
— *Publishers Weekly* (starred review)

*AVAILABLE IN HARDCOVER AND
AUDIO AND AS AN E-BOOK*

★ "Written as witty, off-the-cuff journal entries, this inviting novel takes preadolescent angst and doses it with pure heart."
— *Publishers Weekly* (starred review)

*AVAILABLE IN HARDCOVER
AND AS AN E-BOOK*

www.candlewick.com